Tulsa Trespass
The Tulsa Series #3
Norma Jean Lutz

Tulsa Trespass

ISBN: Print: 978-1-947397-51-4

Tulsa Trespass originally published by Barbour Publishing, Inc., 1997.

Copyright © 2017 by NUWSLink, Inc. and Norma Jean Lutz.

Table of Contents

Note from The Author
Regarding the Tulsa Series

The 4-title Tulsa series has had a long and interesting journey. In the late 1990s, I had just completed the last of four contemporary romance novels for Barbour Publishing's *Heartsong* line. At that time, I was approached by my editor at Barbour to submit ideas to him for historical fiction.

Because I've lived in the Tulsa area for most of my adult life, I knew a little bit about the infamous Tulsa Race Riot of 1921. But honestly, at that time, no one talked much about it. (That later changed as survivors began to speak up.) I knew that that event would serve as the backdrop for my historical, Christian, Tulsa series.

The very same day that my editor asked me for historical fiction ideas, I sat down and wrote out thumbnail sketches for all four titles. He liked the ideas and offered a 4-book contract.

All four, then, were originally published through Barbour's *Heartsong* line where they enjoyed immense popularity. (I still have file folders full of fan letters.)

Later, when the idea of eBooks was in its infancy, an independent group offered to publish my series digitally. As often happens in the publishing industry, the whole thing fell apart due to 1) being ahead of the curve regarding digitally-produced books, and 2) poor business management.

And, yes, yet another group purporting to be an independent publisher, also had their hands in the pie. That too fell apart.

Discouraging to say the least.

The Tulsa Series languished until I recently resurrected them and placed them on Amazon's Kindle. Even with that, little was done to promote the titles.

But this is a new day!

Presently, the four titles are decked out in delightful new covers, plus all will now be available in both print *and* digitally.

I trust as a reader, you will enjoy these stories as much as I enjoyed researching and writing them.

You can connect with me here:

normajean@beanovelist.com

http://www.beanovelist.com/

https://www.facebook.com/BeANovelist/

http://www.cleanteenreads.net/

https://www.facebook.com/CleanTeenReadsNet/

NUWS Link, Inc. Publishing

8703-R. North Owasso Expressway

Ste. 143

Owasso, OK 74055

Chapter 1

Tessa Jurgen pulled her hankie from the pocket of her green-striped Halliburton-Abbott smock and patted the perspiration from her forehead. The ceiling fans above her turned lazily, seemingly a joke as they gave no relief from the sweltering heat. Normally, she enjoyed the aromas of crisp new fabrics from the bolts of cloth on the shelves, but in the dead, hot August air, the musty odor was overpowering.

The customer on the other side of the counter, Mrs. Drake, was one Tessa preferred not to wait on. The woman was hopelessly indecisive. Her simple housedress hung on her limply and the artificial flowers in her brimless toque hat looked as lifeless as Tessa felt. Mrs. Drake hadn't even bothered to arrange the veil.

At her customer's request, Tessa reached up to pull down a large bolt of pink tissue gingham, which was nearly as big as she was. As the bolt hit the wooden counter with a slam, Mrs. Drake was already shaking her head.

"Oh no, no, Miss Jurgen." Rubbing the cloth between her fingers, she said, "This will never do. Too thin. Much too thin. My Sue Lynn likes fabric with more substance for her school dresses." She scanned the rows of bolts lining the shelves behind Tessa. "Let me see the printed voile. There, the one with the pink flowers against the green background."

"Yes, ma'am. Printed voile coming up." Again, she strained to pull down the bolt without dropping it from sheer weight. A sharp pain stabbed through her arm reminding her of the bullet wound she'd received during the Tulsa riot three months ago.

Gaven had told her she shouldn't be lifting so much weight, but she had to work somewhere. She might be engaged to Gaven MacIntyre, but he wasn't supporting her yet.

Again Mrs. Drake tested the fabric by rubbing it between her fingers. "Mmm. Better. Both the same price?"

"Both are forty-nine cents a yard, Mrs. Drake." Tessa shifted from one foot to the other, her feet feeling hot and sweaty in the heavy oxfords. Absently she fingered the strand of pearls at her neck.

Mrs. Drake pulled a McCall's dress pattern from her shopping bag. Pausing a minute, she used the pattern envelope as a fan. "Goodness. This frightful heat. I'll be thankful to see fall get here." After giving a couple more waves, she studied the back of the pattern. "Figure number two with the gathered skirt calls for about four yards."

Out of the corner of her eye, Tessa saw her black friend, Chloe Franklin, walk slowly into the dry goods department staying well out of the way of all the white customers. Tessa gave her a smile and Chloe smiled back.

"Well, Miss Jurgen? Are you going to measure my fabric or not? I said four yards."

"Oh, yes ma'am. Four yards." Tessa deftly unrolled the bolt, measuring each yard against the brass ruler fastened to the edge of the wooden counter. "Will you need thread?" Tessa asked as she cut the piece of fabric and folded it neatly.

"Let me think." Mrs. Drake resumed her fanning with the pattern. "I can't remember whether I have any spools of green."

The floor superintendent, Ila Taylor, came strolling through the department, keys jingling from the belt of her dark high-throated dress. Tessa watched as she stepped up to Chloe to tell her to move over out of the way. Chloe picked up her heavy shopping bag and moved further back. Tessa clenched her teeth to keep from speaking out. Grabbing the sales pad, she quickly figured the price of the fabric and scribbled the numbers.

"Do you need thread?" Tessa asked again, her mind still on Chloe. Before the race riot destroyed most of the black business district of Greenwood a few months ago, Chloe and her friends would never have shopped at the Halliburton-Abbott department store. But now their own stores were gone. Burned.

"You just asked me about the thread, Miss Jurgen. Is the heat getting to you?"

Tessa pulled out her hankie again to touch her face. "Perhaps it is, Mrs. Drake. What did you say about the thread?"

"I said I can't remember if I have green thread at home or not."

Tessa lifted the glass top on the Coats and Clark thread case and selected a spool which matched the fabric and set it on the folded cloth. "Here, Mrs. Drake. As much as you sew for your daughter, you can't have too many spools of green thread, now can you?"

Mrs. Drake chuckled. "I suppose you're right, Miss Jurgen. What a good little sales girl you are. And now let's look at trim. Shall I use lace or rick-rack?" She browsed the case of trim continuing to fan with the pattern package.

"Rick rack would be much more practical for a school dress, don't you think," Tessa suggested as she added the price of thread to the sales slip.

"Oh, you are a dear. Of course, you're right. I need two yards of rick rack. And I think I'll use pink."

Completing the sale, Tessa entered the numbers into the cash register and pulled down the handle to ring up the sale. The drawer flew open with a cling.

After Mrs. Drake left, Chloe took a step to approach the counter when another customer came up in need of a dress zipper. Tessa glanced over at her and gave a slight shrug. Chloe shook her head slowly as if to say it didn't matter. But Tessa wondered if her friend ever got used to such treatment.

At last, the counter was cleared and Tessa motioned to Chloe. "Hurry before someone else comes," she said.

"A body can't hardly hurry in this heat," she said. Her shopping bag appeared to be almost full. "How's the job coming along?" Chloe wanted to know.

"I'm thankful to even have a job, but I'd much rather be teaching. How're Lucie and Wesley?"

"They don't like they new nanny much at all. Nice lady named Mrs. Dunbar. When you was there, Tessa, you was making headway with that contrary little Wesley. Now he acting just like he did before. Trouble, trouble all the time. And little Lucie, she be so sullen. Mrs. Dunbar try her best, but it ain't easy."

Tessa nodded. Her job as governess for the Patton children was terminated the day she befriended Chloe's son, Jasper, when he was in jail. But Tessa was never sorry, since later the boy had been lynched by an angry mob—just days before the riot.

"There's to be another meeting tonight with the attorneys," Chloe said, lowering her voice to a mere whisper. "Will you and Gaven be there?"

Tessa nodded. She was amazed at the giddy feeling which came up in her midsection at the sound of Gaven's name. The strange sensation seemed to well up out of nowhere. "We'll be there. Gaven says if we know what the attorneys say about the pending cases, we can better speak out at the city council meetings."

"You sure gots you a sweet fella in that Gaven. His heart's big as all outdoors. But it took meeting you for him to discover all that love he gots."

"And so, Chloe, just what colors of embroidery thread are you looking for?" Tessa said, raising her voice a level as Ila Taylor sauntered by. She eyed Tessa and Chloe with a critical, calloused expression.

"Variegated. Most definitely variegated." Chloe pointed to the case lined with loops of the colorful threads. "Lavenders and pinks be my all-time favorites."

After the coast was clear, Tessa lowered her voice again. "I know I have a wonderful man in Gaven," she said. "But sometimes I wonder if he's gotten much of a catch in me. Look at me, just a plain old dry-goods clerk in a department store." She touched her strand of pearls at her throat which had been a special gift from Gaven.

"If I wasn't in the presence of all these white folk, I'd turn you 'cross my lap and give you a sound switching for that kind of talk. You the best thing what ever happened to that Gaven boy. He knows it—now you needs to get it into your little noggin as well."

Tessa smiled. "Thanks Chloe. You're exactly what I need." She opened the case to return the embroidery thread.

"Say there. Bring that thread on back out here."

"You really did need embroidery thread?"

"Might sound silly in the face of all we gots to do." She shook her head. "But since I lost all my pretties in the fire, I says to myself, 'Chloe, just making one little pretty is gonna make you feel a whole heap better.'" A soft chuckle bubbled up. "So toss in a set of embroidery hoops girl, and I'm gonna get these old fingers busy."

As if those fingers weren't constantly busy in the kitchen at the Patton mansion, and now in a much larger degree, those hands were helping to rebuild the Greenwood district of Tulsa.

After Chloe left, Floy from housewares came to relieve Tessa for lunch. Floy was a dimpled, vivacious girl with a mop of curly brunette hair and a mouthful of chewing gum. Each morning the hair was perfectly arranged in orderly finger waves beneath her tight-fitting cloche hat. By afternoon the curls were all askew.

"I don't see how you stand the smell of all this fabric," she said wrinkling her turned-up nose as she popped the chewing gum. "I hope

I don't sell any more than a paper of pins while you're gone. I sure don't want to drag down one of those heavy bolts."

"It's not been very busy. You may get your wish."

"Anything you need me to do while you're gone?" she asked, working the gum a little harder.

"I can't think of anything. Just hold the fort."

Thankful for the short respite, Tessa removed her smock, folded it and placed it on a shelf under the counter. She decided to get out of the store and run down the street to Kress's lunchroom for a sandwich.

Out on the street the heavy heat pressed down over her like a scratchy wool blanket. When Tessa still lived back in the Sasakwa Hills, she could run into the woods and wade in the streams to ward off the summer heat, but not here. Not in the city.

As she turned the corner of Fifth and Main she noticed a large sign in the window of Seidenbach's which said: "Back to Pre-War Prices." She stared at it a moment and wondered who ever thought about the Great War now that it was 1921. She certainly didn't. Shimmery waves of heat rose up from the sidewalk as she crossed Main and hurried down to the five-and-dime. In the center of the store, wide steps led down to the basement which was somewhat cooler than out on the street.

"What'll it be today, Tessa?" asked Marvin, the young man behind the counter as he adjusted his white paper hat.

Tessa hopped up on one of the red padded swivel stools, and scanned the menu on the wall. What she really wanted was a sandwich and a cold malted milk, but her money wouldn't stretch that far. Even though she lived at the home of her friend, Pauline Walsh, pennies were still tight. With each paycheck she paid a little for her room and board, and sent a portion home to Mama.

"Just a ham sandwich, Marvin," Tessa said, "with plenty of lettuce. And a glass of ice water."

"Coming up."

Once in a while the memories of her own private garage apartment, which was tucked behind the Patton mansion, flooded Tessa's mind. How she missed that privacy, and having her own little kitchen. The few months she spent there were happy ones.

Life with the busy Walsh family was comfortable enough though, and she had no room to complain. She at least had a place to sleep and food to eat, which was more than most of Chloe's friends and neighbors had.

The lunchroom wasn't crowded since most Tulsa citizens knew better than to come downtown in the mid-day heat. After Marvin

set her sandwich down, he stepped into the kitchen area. Tessa returned thanks for her food, then bit into the thick sandwich. As she thought of the long hot afternoon stretching before her, soft voices from a nearby booth behind her broke into her thoughts. Two ladies were whispering, but Tessa, unfortunately, could hear every word clearly.

"That's the one. That's the girl," said a rather high squeaky voice.

A deeper honeyed voice drawled the answer, "I thought so. I hear the Pattons fired her flat out."

"Kicked her right out on the street, I was told."

Tessa's cheeks burned. In vain, she attempted to shut out the voices. The ham sandwich went dry in her mouth.

"Imagine her walking right into that courthouse, right up to that jail cell to spend time with those colored boys."

"Tsk, tsk," clucked the squeaky voice. "Such audacity. I understand Trevalene Patton was distraught for weeks over the nasty episode."

"Well, she's back now from summer holiday and feeling more fit. She's determined to throw herself into the relief work for those suffering blacks."

My my. Such nobleness after the atrocities all those militant blacks committed."

"Noble. Most noble," cooed the honeyed voice.

"What about the poor daughter—what's her name?"

"Sadella."

"Sadella Patton, yes. The one who was accosted in the alley by those colored boys. What have you heard about her?"

"After a nightmare experience like that? Who knows. She may never be quite herself ever again."

Stomach churning, Tessa slid down off the stool.

"Tessa," Marvin said, coming out of the kitchen. "You've left half a sandwich."

"I'm too hot to eat," was all she could say as she hurried out of the lunchroom, not wanting to even glance back to see who spoke such hate-filled words.

Chapter 2

At quitting time, Tessa entered the noisy third-floor cloak room, folded her smock and placed it in her locker. The cloak room was situated just off the employees' lounge. From the rack in the corner she fetched her ribboned straw hat and worked the hat pin through the braids atop her head, fastening it in place, then grabbed her handbag. Tonight she would ask Mina Walsh if she could pack a lunch tomorrow. Eating with others in the employee lunch room would be better than Kress's lunch counter—and cheaper as well.

"Are you going to the trolley stop, Tessa?" Floy asked as she took her cloche hat from the rack and firmed it on her head. "Or is that good-looking boyfriend of yours picking you up?"

"How can you bear to wear that hat in this heat?" Tessa wanted to know.

Floy's small handbag hung on a long gold chain which she slung over her shoulder. Working her gum and making it pop, she said, "Cloche hats are the absolute rage, Tessa. Everyone's wearing them. Who cares about the heat? Fashion reigns supreme." Her mischievous eyes twinkled. "So what about the boyfriend?"

"Gaven's working late at Skelly. He's picking me up later."

"Good. Let's walk to the trolley together."

Floy had befriended Tessa since her very first day at Halliburton-Abbott, showing her around and introducing her to the other employees. Now as they left, the bubbly girl hailed good-bye to nearly every employee by their first names.

Floy was small in size like Tessa. Not as short as Tessa's five foot, but close. It was comfortable to walk with her. "Did you have a black customer today?" Floy asked as they pushed out the front doors with the others.

"Yes I did. Why do you ask?"

They stopped together at the traffic light on the corner of Fifth and Boston. "I just happened to overhear Ila Taylor saying something to Mr. Osborn about your helping a black woman and taking way too long to do it."

"I appreciate your telling me. I'll be more careful."

"She knows about... Well, you know. About what happened during the riot."

"That I was in Greenwood the night it happened?" The light changed and they crossed together. "I guess most people in Tulsa know. It's certainly no secret." She could feel her voice getting tight as though she had to defend her actions. If Chloe had not taken her in after the Pattons fired her and kicked her out of the garage apartment, she would have had no place to go.

"No need to get testy with me," Floy said, dimples flashing. "Personally, I think you're a daring heroine. Almost like Mary Pickford in *Tess of the Storm Country*. Think of that—Tess, Tessa. Why you even *look* like Mary—tiny and with beautiful golden hair."

Tessa had to laugh at this comparison to a moving-picture starlet. She and Gaven went to see a moving picture once, and indeed the dynamic Mary Pickford was starring. "I'm hardly a daring heroine, Floy, but thanks for the compliment. And I'm sorry if I was short with you. Sometimes I feel as though the entire city is talking about me behind my back."

"A few yes. The entire city, no. Many people in Tulsa admire the stand you took."

"If that's true, they must all be tongue-tied."

At the trolley stop, they escaped the glaring sun by standing beneath a nearby shade tree.

"It was that mammoth Klan march last spring that frightened most of the citizens. Then the lynchings, and finally the riot. It's enough to quiet anyone from talking too much. Anyway, there's my trolley. I'll see you tomorrow."

"Bye, Floy. And thanks again," Tessa called out as Floy stepped out to catch the trolley which would take her north of the city.

In a moment or two, hers came along, which would take her south to Norfolk Street. As it came to a stop, Pauline came scurrying up Elgin at a fast pace. The conductor saw her and kindly waited a bit. He knew most of his regular riders.

"It's much too warm for you to hurry, Pauline," Tessa warned as they stepped up and paid their fares. "You'll have heat stroke for sure."

"I just hurried the last block—after I looked up and saw you standing there," she said between heavy breaths. "I thought how nice it would be ride home together."

Pauline was a large quiet girl, whom Tessa could easily envision living on a farm and milking cows. Her kindness and that of her family's had seen Tessa through difficult times. Pauline worked the switchboard at the telephone office. Some weeks she worked an evening shift, but this week she was on days.

Hot air blew through the windows on them, as the little car clanged its way down Elgin Street. As they chatted about the day's events, Tessa considered sharing about the conversation she'd heard in the lunchroom, then thought better of it. Instead she resolved to put it out of her mind completely. "Consider the source," Chloe would have said.

"Will you be helping us with the relief efforts at the church this evening," Pauline asked, "or are you and Gaven going over to Greenwood?"

"Since he's working late, he told me to go to the church and he'd pick me up there."

"Good. We can ride to the church together after supper. Seems like Gaven's always working late. Are the oil leasing offices that busy?"

"Gaven says leases needing to be processed are stacked to the ceiling. The pay is good, but he'd much rather be in the classroom teaching."

"Just like you, right?" Pauline said.

Tessa gave a little sigh. She tried so hard not to be despondent that she was no longer teaching, but she missed it terribly. "Just like me," she answered simply.

The Walshes lived in a comfortable little bungalow in a friendly neighborhood at the end of the trolley line. When the girls arrived home, they quickly washed and gave Mina a hand with supper preparations. Time and again Mina commented how good it was to have extra help, although Tessa never felt she did that much.

She went to the sideboard in the dining room to bring out the dishes to set the table. On top the sideboard were several large photos of a handsome square-jawed young man dressed in the stiff-collared uniform of an army officer. The Walsh's son, Wayne, had given his life on the battlefields of France during the war. The tragic loss worked to draw Tessa and Pauline closer since Tessa had lost her younger brother, Berg, to pneumonia a few years earlier.

Tessa still thought about Berg and grieved. As children growing up they'd been almost inseparable. The loss of her father, on the other hand, affected her quite differently. When he was shot by a fellow bootlegger last spring, his death was almost a relief for Tessa and her family. Now her younger sisters Siegrid and Vega, along with Mama, were safe in the home of Pastor Stedman.

"Ho there," a booming voice broke into her thoughts. "How's our little love bird this evening?" It was Pauline's father, Russell, who'd just come in from work. He spent long hours out in the heat keeping the electrical system of the trolley lines working smoothly. His tanned, jovial face was etched with laugh lines.

Tessa felt a blush creep to her ears. His teasing reminded her of Pastor Stedman whom she'd lived with when she taught school near the Glenn Pool. "I'm fine, Mr. Walsh," she answered. "Did you have a good day?"

"It'll be a better day when you remember you can call me Russ. And it'll be a better day when this infernal heat lets up. Had one of my men faint dead away this afternoon. Just conked out cold on the concrete." He shook his head as he headed toward the stairs to go up and wash. "I didn't know whether to slosh a bucket of water on him, or administer a whiff of smelling salts."

Tessa chuckled at his comments. Mina came in carrying a platter of fried chicken. "Hurry now, Russ. Everything's almost ready."

Midway up the stairs, he stopped and said, "My men would never believe how you boss me around."

Mina smiled and shook her head. "Isn't he a sight?" she said to Tessa.

"A sight you seem to enjoy very much," Pauline said as she followed on her mother's heels. She placed a bowl heaping with fluffy mashed potatoes, and the brimming gravy boat, side by side on the table.

"You weren't supposed to notice," her mother replied.

This friendly bantering, full of love, went on continually, giving Tessa a sense of peace and belonging.

Once they were all seated, and Russ had prayed over the food, he said to Tessa, "I've decided that when you and Gaven get married you two can just live in our upstairs. I'm getting used to your cute little face at our dinner table."

"Now Russ, no fair teasing our guest," Mina said as she passed around the fried okra. Turning to Tessa she said, "But he's right. With Gail married and gone, and after losing Wayne, the house seems empty."

"Never fear, Mother," Pauline quipped. "From the looks of things, I'll be here for quite a while."

"Don't listen to her, Mina," Tessa countered. "I've seen how that new young man at church has been looking at her."

Now it was Pauline's turn to blush, which pleased Tessa.

"Hey, you didn't know? I've already given him ten bucks to ask her out," Russ said, laughing richly.

"Oh Daddy, please." But Pauline laughed as well.

"Tell us Russ," Mina jumped in to change the subject, "how are the repairs coming along in the riot area?"

"You never saw such a mess. Tessa's been there. She knows."

Tessa nodded. "Gaven calls it a war zone." And her darling Gaven, who'd fought in France as Wayne Walsh had, would know.

"It'll be another month or more before the lines are all restored. Should have been finished a month ago, but city hall's dragging its feet. They're giving us fits with all the red tape. Worse than dealing with Washington D.C. Now what could be so difficult about processing the work orders, I'd like to know."

"Unless someone somewhere with some amount of money didn't want them to be processed. More potatoes, Daddy?" Pauline passed the bowl to her father.

"You don't want to be making remarks like that too loudly on the streets of Tulsa, Pauline," her father warned, "but I'm afraid you may be right."

"Those poor people." Mina shook her head. "I'm pleased that you girls are lending a hand in the relief efforts. I was down at the church this afternoon myself for a while. But it still seems so little when so much is needed."

Tessa agreed. The horrific days and nights of burning and looting of the black district had affected thousands of black families. She wondered how they would ever survive the winter.

Soon after supper dishes were finished, Tessa and Pauline caught the trolley to the Boulder Street Church. As they rode together in quiet, Tessa remembered the New Year's Eve watch party at the church where she'd first spent time with Gaven. How new everything had been back then. The glittering city, and the large church were much different from the rural area where grew up. But now she'd become accustomed to all that Tulsa had to offer—both the good and the bad. And best of all was Gaven MacIntyre.

The cool interior of the church gave the girls a moment's relief from the heavy heat. They walked downstairs to the basement, which had been turned into a reception center for donations for those affected by the riots. Distribution had slowed from what it had been just after the riot in June, but there was still much to do.

They were greeted by the other ladies who were already busy sorting and then recording the donated items of canned foods, clothing, and linens. Pauline and Tessa were assigned to a side room where they separated piles of clothing into groups of men's, women's, and children's, and hung them on long racks donated by one of the department stores. Two other ladies sat at a nearby table, mending torn clothing and replacing missing buttons.

It crossed Tessa's mind that the husbands of some of these women working with the relief efforts, may have been the very ones who torched and looted the houses and businesses in Greenwood that night. There was no way of knowing, since hundreds had taken part in the mob violence. It was senseless to dwell on such negative thoughts, since it tended to feed her anger. Sometimes she won out in her battle against bitterness, other times she failed miserably.

She had been working for about an hour when Gaven swept into the room, and everything lit up. He was in his shirtsleeves with his tie loosened. His hat was pushed to the back of his head and the dark brown curls were all tousled on his forehead. Suddenly there came that bubbly feeling from deep inside her at the sight of him striding across the room—as though no one else in the world existed or mattered but her. He answered the greetings from the others, but his soft brown eyes were on Tessa.

"I'm sorry to be so late," he said taking off his hat and reaching out for her hand. His hand felt strong, secure, safe.

"It's all right."

"I hope we haven't missed too much of the meeting. Hello Pauline."

"Hello to you too, Gaven MacIntyre. Nice of you to notice me over here in the corner."

Gaven reddened. "Of course I noticed you. Sorry to take your work partner away. Do you have a way home?"

"I'm sure one of the ladies can take me. Don't worry about it. You two go on."

As they turned to leave the room, Tessa paused as she heard a loud familiar voice out in the main workroom. "Now that I've returned," the voice said in an authoritative tone, "I've taken over the total supervision for the relief activities. It's been a misdirected hodgepodge up till now. But I'm here to remedy that problem as quickly as possible."

Gaven and Tessa emerged from the side room to come face to face with the cold gaze of Mrs. Trevalene Patton.

Chapter 3

"I might've known I'd find you here," Trevalene said in her deep southern drawl. She looked straight at Tessa from behind the veil of her plum-colored, broad-brimmed hat. Her bulging figure was closely fit, probably with the aid of a cinched corset, into a matching plum silk dress trimmed in delicate lace cuffs and collar. She clutched her large pocketbook in gloved hands as though someone threatened to snatch it from her.

"I suppose you're here to assuage your guilt for all the trouble you caused. If only you had done as Mr. Patton and I suggested. If only you never would have gone to visit that wretched nigra boy in jail..." She paused a moment as though to compose herself. "All this might never have happened."

The needless dramatics gave Tessa a slow burn. How dare she act innocent when it was her own daughter who sent Jasper Franklin to his death? Gaven obviously sensed her anger as he squeezed her hand tightly.

"If you'll excuse us, Mrs. Patton, we're in a terrible hurry," he said. And with that he steered her around the confrontation and out the door.

"I don't blame you for not wanting to hear the truth, Mr. MacIntyre," Trevalene said raising her voice—but the words faded as Gaven practically dragged Tessa up the stairs and out to his waiting roadster.

"Thank you," she managed to say as they drove north on Boulder toward Greenwood. "No telling what I might have said if you hadn't been there."

He turned to her, smiling. "I sensed a little volcano was about to explode."

"I'm not so sure it would have been little. How dare she twist the truth to suit her purposes?"

"Just be patient. People like Mrs. Patton usually cause their own demise."

"But she has so much clout in the city. I caught a glimpse of it today at lunch." Briefly, she related the conversation she'd overheard at Kress's lunch counter. "From what they said, you'd think they approved of everything Trevalene says and does.

"I'm sorry you had to hear all that," Gaven said, reaching over to take her hand. "I know it's not easy, but try to keep it in perspective. You heard the opinions of two women—rather loose-lipped women at that—not the whole town."

Of course he was right. She had over-reacted. But everything around her seemed broiling in a state of agitation and unrest ever since the riot. Would people's heated emotions ever simmer down?

"Anyway, I have a bit of good news that should cheer you up." His voice lifted and his eyes smiled at her.

Tessa knew Gaven had signed his contract with the Tulsa School System to teach sixth grade again at Riverview in September, so she couldn't imagine what the good news was about. "Does the good news concern you?"

"In a round about way. Because now that you're wearing my engagement ring, everything that concerns you concerns me as well."

Tessa glanced down at the pearl and ruby ring she wore on her right hand. Come next January that ring would become her wedding ring and be switched to the other hand. "So it concerns me then?"

He nodded. "I ran into my English professor from Kendall College today. Dr. Edward Misek is his name. He and I always hit it off. Not because I was so keen in composition you understand, but because he just seemed to like me."

"And?"

"And I told him about you."

"What in the world would you tell a college professor about me?"

"Why, I told him how badly you wanted to get your degree, of course."

Tessa was quiet for a moment. She'd never actually expressed her longing to Gaven, and yet he knew. He seemed to sense it the very first time he drove her to the Kendall campus and showed her around. Almost as though he could read her heart, and it made her feel full to bursting with love for him.

"I explained about your taking the county exam in Creek County and the teaching experience you've had at the Independence School. I must say he seemed impressed."

"Impressed by what? Hundreds of teachers in the state use a county certificate."

Gaven turned the roadster down Archer next to the Sand Springs Railroad Line. "You're right, but he's impressed that you're not satisfied to stay in that position. He wants you to come to his office and take a few tests."

Tessa's heart gave a little jump. "What kind of tests?"

"The entrance exam, I believe. He said if you do well on that, he would look into the possibility of a scholarship for you. What do you think of that?"

"Why I'm terrified...*and* excited." How blessed she was to have a future husband who wasn't threatened by her desire to study and learn.

Gaven laughed. "No need to be terrified. You'll do fine. Just fine."

"Will you help me? You still have your college books, don't you?"

He took his eyes off the road to glance at her. "You don't need to ask twice. What I need is another excuse to spend more time with you." He gave her hand a squeeze. "I'll have evenings free once school starts. And I'll be so relieved to get out of the clutches of the Skelly Oil Company."

"And I thought you were grateful for those good wages."

"Look who's talking to a fellow about money. The girl who gave up her good job to help Jasper Franklin. Well, I don't mind letting go of the oil money to get myself back into the classroom—that's where I belong."

The classroom. That's where Tessa belonged as well. But in Tulsa she'd have to have a degree in order to get there. Now it looked as though that might be an attainable dream.

Driving through the burned-out sections of the Greenwood district never failed to depress Tessa, no matter how many times she saw it. The entire stretch of the main business district, all in rubble. Neighborhoods destroyed.

It affected Gaven the same way, she could tell. Once he had said, "It reminds me so much of the war. The sight makes me want to jump into the trenches with my rifle ready."

After a full two months, there were few if any signs of major rebuilding. Instead, hundreds of tents had been erected. A few tents had floors of brick or lumber salvaged from the wreckage, the others sported dirt floors where the residents lived from day to day with only the bare necessities.

The meeting that evening was held in a large tent down from the corner of Greenwood and Archer, and it was well under way when Gaven and Tessa arrived. Tessa was pleased to see a few white faces interspersed among the black ones. There were those who truly cared what happened here.

Attorney Miles Calbert was addressing the group. Miles and his co-workers had worked tirelessly through the long hot summer, fighting to counteract ordinance after ordinance spewing out of city hall. This in spite of the fact that his own office on Greenwood Street lay in ruins.

The meeting stopped momentarily as the black leaders paused to greet Gaven and Tessa and arrange chairs for them in their midst. There was Chloe and her husband, Willard, along with Preacher Sam and his wife Mama Sue. A number of other familiar faces smiled at them in welcome. Pole Williamson was there, the butler and chauffeur for the Pattons, and Elsie Mae who worked in the Patton's laundry.

"When the Fire Ordinance first came forth," Miles was saying, "we went directly into action to file suit. The contrived ordinance stated that any structure in the area must be constructed of concrete, brick or steel, and had to be at least two stories high. This obviously was a thinly-veiled attempt to stop any of us from rebuilding our homes here."

Miles pulled out his white handkerchief and mopped his brow as he shuffled papers with his other hand. "This case was taken before district court on August sixth. I'm pleased to be able to announce to you this evening that three judges in district court declared this ordinance void!" His voice rose to a crescendo as the little group burst into cheers and hearty applause.

"This is a landmark," Miles went on when the exuberance subsided. "This gives us hope that the mayor and his so-called committees will realize we aren't going to give in without a fight." Another cheer went up.

"What about the aid that's being offered?" Preacher Sam wanted to know. "I hears from my kinfolk in Illinois that the *Chicago Tribune* offered aid. What's happening?"

"As far as we can ascertain," Miles told the group, "offers have come in from across the nation, but the Chamber of Commerce is refusing the aid."

Whispers of surprise buzzed through the still, hot air beneath the tent's canopy.

"Don't we got nothing to say about it?" Mama Sue asked. "We be the ones who needs the help."

Miles shook his head. "This is one area where I have no grounds. The statement given out from city hall and the chamber is that Tulsa is to blame for the problems, and she will take care of her own."

"My my," Mama Sue said shaking her head. "If only that were true."

"Where do we have leverage?" Gaven spoke up.

The word "we" spoke volumes to Tessa. She could remember when her fiancé was warning her against forming close friendships with the blacks. Now he was right here by her side.

Miles again was shuffling through his papers. "Let me review where we now stand and what's left to be done. First, we have the problem of insurance settlements. In spite of all we've done and tried to do, it looks as if no policy will be paying since this is deemed a riot and therefore excluded."

Tessa cringed. Even though she'd heard it said before, at least in earlier meetings, Miles' voice had a ring of optimism. Now he seemed resigned to the fact that this was a lost cause.

"Secondly," he went on, "building permits are dragging at a snail's pace. This we can continue to do something about. More representation at city council meetings is needed. We need to rally more of our people to attend the meetings, in addition to using every legal channel we can find."

"What about the lumber and supplies?" another man asked. "I gots my permit but now the man at the lumber company say he got no lumber for no black man."

Miles turned to his younger colleague, Lanier Elledge. "Lanny has the action plan for that area."

Tessa had been told by Chloe that this young man's wife died in premature childbirth the day after the riot, while he was interned at the fairgrounds along with all the other hundreds of men from Greenwood. His baby died as well.

"We don't have to buy our supplies in this area," Lanny said in a quiet voice. "There are lumber yards in every town from here to Arkansas. If we have to bring supplies in here one brick, one plank, and one nail at a time, we'll do it."

That statement brought yet another rousing cheer. By now other folk had gathered on the grounds about the tent and were listening to the proceedings.

"Tessa knows people around the Glenn Pool," Gaven said. "If we can get a truck, we can purchase supplies there."

Chloe looked over at Tessa. "What about that Hod Latham fellow, Tessa? He still be on the lookout for you."

Tessa wished Chloe weren't quite so vocal. Hod Latham was a name Tessa wanted to forget. "I don't think there's a problem," she replied. She'd heard through Pastor Stedman that Hod had retreated further into the Sasakwa Hills with his bootlegging business going full tilt.

To Chloe, Gaven said, "I'll be there to take care of her."

"Can you make a trip as soon as a week from this Saturday?" Lanier asked Gaven. "We should have a number of orders by then."

Gaven looked at Tessa. "Do you work that Saturday?"

She shook her head. "I have it off."

"It's settled then. We'll go, and whatever it takes after that, just let us know."

Others gave their names, stating where they could go, and when. With a few more bits of business the meeting was concluded. The crowd dispensed with little knots of people standing about in the warm night, swatting mosquitoes and continuing to talk over the issues, daring to plan for the future, which at times seemed terribly bleak. Several came up to shake hands with Gaven and to thank him for his interest and help.

While Gaven talked to the men, Tessa stepped aside to talk to Chloe and tell her the good news about the professor who was interested in her.

Chloe's black eyes lit up at the news. "Now that's what I needs to hear—a morsel of good news for a change. Helps me forget for a minute about all this heartache around here. Can't nobody throw no test at you that you can't handle, girl. You just remember that."

"Thanks for believing in me, Chloe."

She nodded in Gaven's direction. "And you gots another one there who believes same as me. You keep holda that man. Don't never let him go."

"I plan to do exactly that." Tessa watched Gaven for a moment admiring his handsome profile and soft brown eyes. Turning back to Chloe she asked, "What about Jasper's body, Chloe? What have the officials told you?"

"Oh now you know how they is. We done asked about all the times we dare ask about getting his body back to bury. They's so many bodies missing from the night of the riot, it seems a small matter now."

Tessa marveled at Chloe's strength.

"I had to turn loose of it," she continued. "I pray, 'Jesus, show me how to turn loose of it.' Willard and me, we knows where Jasper be at anyhow." Her eyes twinkled. "He be dancing around his mansion, and I hopes he's helping Jesus to get mine ready, too."

At that moment, Gaven came to fetch her as quick good-byes were said and he led her to the car. "Let's stop by my place, and I'll grab a couple of my old textbooks," he told her. "Perhaps the Walshes won't mind if we use the front parlor for a while."

"I'm sure they won't mind."

On the way to the boarding house where Gaven lived, they discussed what had transpired at the meeting, trying to think of other ways they could help break through all the red tape at city hall.

Their minds were on other things as they turned the corner on Baltimore and there in front of the tall three-story house on the shady street sat a silver Kissell sports coupe. Sauntering down the walk from the house back to his car was Shelby Harland.

Chapter 4

"I thought that guy was a thousand miles from Tulsa," Gaven said, not bothering to conceal his disgust.

"Don't be too hard on him, Gaven. Most of the time he means well."

At the sound of Gaven's approaching roadster, Shelby paused and peered through the darkness at them. Then recognizing the car, he gave a cheery wave.

"That guy gets in more trouble by accident than ten people could on purpose. Why would he come back from New York so soon—especially with the Klan hot on his trail?"

"Do you suppose he's here looking for you?" Tessa asked.

"We'll soon find out. Since we've been spotted, I don't guess we can run and hide."

"Oh Gaven. Of course we wouldn't hide."

Shelby, whose father was head of the massive Harland Oil Company, hurried toward them as Gaven parked the roadster at the curb behind the Kissell. Shel was dressed in knickers and a billed tweed cap as though he'd just come from the links at the Tulsa Country Club.

"Hello you two. Gaven, Tessa. Ooh la la, little Tessa—those eyes are as gorgeous blue as ever. What a ripping stroke of luck that you two should just happen by."

"I do happen to live here," Gaven said dryly.

"Well of course. How silly of me." Shelby pulled off his cap and leaned over to peer in the window. Only then did Tessa see how haggard he looked. To have turned the tables on the powerful Ku Klux Klan had put a few worry lines on his face.

"What are you doing here?" Gaven asked.

"Actually, I was looking for Tessa's cousin. Doesn't Erik Torsten live here anymore?"

"Erik moved back to Bartlesville, Shel," she said softly.

"And Clarette?"

"He and Clarette Fortier were married a day or two after you left for New York. I thought you knew."

"A fellow can hope can't he?"

Suddenly, Shelby opened the car door. "Scoot over Tessa. Let's go somewhere where we can talk."

"Sit still, Tessa," Gaven countered. "Listen pal, we had other plans..."

"It wasn't really anything that couldn't wait, Gaven," she said. "We can give him a few minutes." Tessa sensed that Shelby needed to talk.

Gaven released a sigh. "All right. If you say so. Jump aboard, Harland."

"Thanks awfully," he said squeezing in as Tessa scooted over.

Gaven pulled out onto the street. "Where to?" he asked.

"I don't suppose you'd consider one of the choc joints on the edge of town?"

"Shelby Harland!" Tessa spouted. "You know better than that."

"I thought not. What about one of the hotel coffee shops? They should still be open."

Gaven gave him a sidelong glance. "You want the whole town to know you're back?"

"Who cares? They'll know sooner or later anyhow."

Gaven turned a corner and headed the roadster back toward the other side of town. "Let's make it later. Let's take him to the Walsh's, Tessa. They won't mind."

"Good idea."

"Walsh? Who's that?"

"A family who cared enough to take me in after the riot."

"You could have lived at the Harland mansion in style, Miss Jurgen," Shel reminded her.

Tessa knew his invitation which followed her dismissal from the Patton's, was merely one of his whims. Thankfully, she had refused. Even though she lost most of her possessions in the fire and took a bullet in her arm, she was still better off than if she'd taken shelter with the Harlands.

When they arrived, Pauline had already gone to bed. Mina met them at the back door. She didn't so much as raise her brows when she learned their visitor's identity, as though the children of oil barons dropped by every day or so.

"Sorry to bother you, Mina," Gaven told her. "We just need a place to talk for a while."

"Would you prefer the kitchen or the parlor?"

Shelby looked around the homey little kitchen. "I like it here. The kitchen's just fine."

"I was just going on up to bed. You kids make yourselves at home. Tessa you know where the coffee pot is. Help yourself to the cookies in the jar."

"Thank, Mina."

Soon the small cozy kitchen was filled with the sound of the percolator on the stove, and Shelby was munching on Mina's peanut butter cookies.

"So why *did* you come back?" Gaven asked as Tessa poured the steaming coffee.

For herself she fixed a glass of lemonade from the icebox. "We thought you were going to stay away till things cooled off," she said. "Clarette told us you were trying to sell your music to Broadway producers."

Shelby dumped a couple of heaping spoonsful of sugar into his coffee and stirred. Shaking his head, he said, "It's no use. Clarette may have thought I had talent, but no one in New York thought so."

"But you didn't give it time," Gaven said. "It doesn't happen overnight."

"Yeah, I suppose you're right. I even tried to use Dad's influence, but that didn't make much difference in the music industry."

Tessa sat down at the table and looked at Shelby's tired face. The happy-go-lucky derring-do had disappeared. "Shel, what's the *real* problem here? What's the real reason you came back to Tulsa?"

Shel looked at Tessa, then at Gaven. "She's a sharp one, this one."

"I know," Gaven agreed.

"Tessa, you know the times when I flirted with you—of course I thought you were pretty and all—but I was just cutting up. Having fun."

"I knew that."

"But with Clarette..."

"What about Clarette, Shel?" But Tessa didn't even need to ask. The pain was written all over his face.

"For the first time in my life I found I truly loved someone." He looked at them as though searching. "I loved her, but I betrayed her. I caused her to be kidnapped by the Klan. All the way back to Oklahoma on the train, I kept thinking maybe she hadn't married Torsten after all. I almost fooled myself into thinking there was still a chance for me in her life." The slap-dash playboy suddenly buried his face in his hands. "I've been a blind idiot."

Tessa reached over to pat his arm. "We all make mistakes, Shel, but God forgives when we ask Him."

"What difference does it make now? Without Clarette, nothing matters."

"That's not true, Shelby," Gaven put in. "If the Lord has shown you that you have the capacity to love someone deeply, then He'll send along the mate who's right for you. Just wait and see."

Shelby put his hands down. "You make it sound so simple. So easy."

"Gaven doesn't mean right now, Shel. He means after your heart has healed from this awful grief."

"She trusted me," Shel said as though he'd not heard a word they said. "She trusted me and I put her right into their hands. She must hate me. I hate me. Without Clarette, nothing really matters anymore."

"Don't talk like that," Tessa said. "God loves you, Shel. He'll forgive you if you'll just ask. Then He'll help you to forgive yourself."

At that, Shel stood to his feet and grabbed the expensive tweed cap, which he'd tossed on a nearby counter. "Gaven, old man, you've been quite decent to put up with my blubbering." He gave Gaven a firm smack on the shoulder. "And to think how rather nasty I've been to you. I'll thank you to take me back to my car now. I'll get myself out of your hair."

Tessa looked at Gaven. She could see the concern in his eyes. "I'll stay here. You go on home," she told him.

He nodded, as he came around the table to kiss her softly on the forehead. She took his hand and pressed it to her cheek. "I'll call you in the morning before you go to work," he told her. "We'll get those textbooks another evening and study together."

After they left, Tessa wondered what would become of Shelby Harland. The desperation in his eyes gave her an unsettled feeling. Before she fell asleep that night, she said a special prayer for him.

———⊙———

EACH AUGUST DAY WAS hotter and more oppressive than the one before. Some days Tessa felt she was drowning in a sea of fabrics at the store. On one such day, she was measuring bright yellow dotted Swiss for a customer who planned to use it for curtains. Tessa thumped the bolt over and over on the wooden counter as she unrolled the yards of fuzzy cloth. Pausing a moment, she wondered if she was going to pass clean out on the floor.

Just then, from behind her came a small voice. "Miss Jurgen. Hello, Miss Jurgen." Whirling around, Tessa was overjoyed to see Lucie Patton standing off to the side, giving a little wave. Beside her, more reserved, but with excitement sparkling in his eyes, stood her older brother, Wesley.

A rush of joy surged through her at the sight of them and all the awful heat was quite forgotten. "Hello, children!" she said. "Come let me have a look at you. My, how you're growing."

They came running then, grabbing her in wild hugs. Wes pulled off his cap like a gentleman. His impeccable matching jacket and knickerbockers were much too warm for such a hot day.

Behind them stood a matronly lady dressed in a plain navy dress which hung to her ankles, with a worn felt hat that seemed dreadfully out of date. But the smile on her face told Tessa that somehow this older lady understood the situation perfectly.

"Young lady," the impatient customer reminded her, "please finish my order."

"Yes, ma'am. Of course. You children stand out of the way now and I'll be through here in just a minute."

The dotted Swiss was quickly measured, cut, and folded, and the sale rung up. Then she gathered the two of them into her arms.

"When they learned we were coming downtown," the older lady said, "they begged and begged to come find you." Behind her hand, she said, "Mrs. Patton doesn't know."

"I understand," Tessa said. But she was too delighted at seeing the children, she cared nothing about their mother or her spiteful ways.

"This is Mrs. Dunbar. She's our new nanny. You can call her Mattie, but we have to call her Mrs. Dunbar." Lucie's words tumbled one over the other as she clung to Tessa.

Tessa shook hands with Mattie and liked her immediately.

"We miss you, Miss Jurgen," Sadness reflected in Lucie's expressive brown eyes as she twisted one of her long brunette curls. The large bow fastened in the back of her hair matched her ruffled, lacy blue dress which was neatly starched and ironed. "I wish you could come back to us," she said.

"I do too, Lucie, but the Lord had other plans for my life."

"He didn't ask me if I like the plans," Wesley said, his arms folded across his chest.

"He seldom does, Wes. That's because He knows better than we do what's best for our lives."

"We heard you got burned up in the riot," Lucie said, her voice choking on a little sob. "I cried all night long. But when Chloe came back she told us you were safe."

"We went to the ocean," Wesley said. "It was a swell place, but it would've been better if you'd been there with us."

His words touched her heart. This from the boy Tessa didn't think she could ever win over. His sensitivity was still intact. Hopefully, it would remain that way.

"I had my birthday while we were away. I'm eight now." Lucie glanced over at her brother. "And Wesley will be eleven next month."

"You're both growing so fast I can hardly believe it," Tessa told them.

Wesley took a step closer and lowered his voice. "Mrs. Dunbar isn't a fun teacher like you."

Tessa smiled. "That's a fine compliment and I thank you for it, Wes. But if you're going to be running your own airport someday, and flying those airplanes across the sky, your education must be of utmost importance—no matter who's teaching."

Wes stood a little straighter. "I'm going to fly. I just *have* to."

"I know you will. And I know you'll continue to study as hard for Mrs. Dunbar as you did for me."

"Mother's gone almost all the time now." Lucie nudged closer like a little puppy.

"Helping with the relief work she says," Wesley added.

"And Miss Jurgen, you know what?" Lucie's eyes were wide.

"What?"

"Mother told Chloe not to be talking to us so much, but she does anyway." Lucie smiled, spreading her little hands for emphasis. "Chloe says nobody's gonna tell her what to say or who to say it to!"

"That's because Chloe loves you," Tessa said.

"We gotta love her more, now that Jasper's gone," Lucie added.

"You're a very smart little girl," Tessa said. And she meant it.

Another customer interrupted the glad reunion. "I must get back to work." She hugged them both one more time. "Thank you, Mattie, for letting them come." More softly, she added, "If Trevalene ever found out, you could be in a great deal of trouble."

Mattie tilted her chin as she adjusted her black handbag on her arm. "I don't worry much about Trevalene Patton."

After they left, Tessa felt much better about the children and their well-being. Their visit had revitalized her, giving her the energy to finish out the day.

Her feet were aching by the time quitting time finally came. What a blessing to see Gaven standing at the front entrance waiting for her. She immediately told him all about the visit from the children. His wide smile told her how pleased he was for her.

As he led her to his roadster, an open coupe full of noisy, shouting young people careened down Main Street. Gaven grabbed her arm. "Tessa, look!"

Tessa looked up to see Sadella Patton at the wheel of the speeding coupe, and snuggled close beside her was Shelby Harland.

Tessa's hand flew to her mouth in surprise. "Oh no," she whispered. "Please, Lord. Not that!"

Chapter 5

Tessa bounced around on the hard seat of the flatbed truck as they rumbled down the dusty road toward the Glenn Pool. Gaven wrestled with the steering wheel, trying to avoid the deepest ruts. Pastor Stedman and Edith, along with Mama and the girls were excited about their arrival and Edith was planning a big dinner. Tessa could hardly wait to see them all again. How she hoped they would like Gaven—but then how could they help but like him, as wonderful as he was.

The countryside was dying from the heat and lack of rain; only the hardiest of wildflowers sported any color. In another few weeks, the fall rains would come and bring much-needed relief. Hopefully, a few of the houses in Greenwood would go up before then. And especially before the first cold spell. Tessa couldn't stand to think of the little children with no homes through the cold winter months.

But today was too nice a day to think sad thoughts. Her heart was soaring as they traveled along. She hadn't been this happy since before Berg died. No matter how mean Papa acted or talked, Berg had the ability to dispel the fear and awfulness of the situation. His way of making his sisters laugh helped them forget their troubles. Even Mama couldn't help laughing at Berg's antics.

She looked over at Gaven to study his gentle face. He too had a way of dispelling the awfulness of a situation. As they bounced along, Gaven began to sing. His clear baritone floated up above the noise of the clattering old truck. She joined in on the ones she knew. Then he had the bright idea that they would sing rounds. Before too many more miles had passed, they were hopelessly reduced to peals of laughter and giggles. Tessa's sides ached from laughing and Gaven could barely keep control of the truck.

"It's so good to hear you laugh," he said. They had just approached Lone Grove Crossroads just north of the Glenn Pool. "When I first met you, you were terribly serious."

"I was facing some pretty serious matters when you met me," she reminded him as she dabbed at her laugh-tears with a hankie.

"That's true. But you're not alone anymore. I'm going to be right here to take care of you."

Tessa let his words soak deep into her subconscious like raindrops on her parched and thirsty soul.

"There's the lumberyard where we'll pick up the supplies on our way home." She pointed out the building as they drove through the abbreviated main intersection of town. The whole town boasted only a handful of businesses. "And there's Hargis' Mercantile. Clyde Hargis serves on the school board. He was one who didn't think I could teach when he first saw me."

"But you changed his mind."

Tessa like the way he put it. "Yes, I guess I did. I proved I could handle the children."

From town, she directed him down the dusty country roads that were little more than graded trails, past the fields of oil derricks where the pounding of the pumping rigs continued day and night; past the one-room school where she'd taught for two years; past the farm houses of the neighbors she'd come to know while she served as their teacher.

"It's just over the next little hill," Tessa told him, with excitement building in her voice. When she lived with the Stedmans, Pastor used to drive her home to their cabin in the hills nearly every weekend. Now she'd not seen her Mama or sisters since her father's funeral the previous spring.

As they topped the next ridge, there it was—the two-story white-frame parsonage situated adjacent to the small rural church where the Stedmans pastored. Tessa had never seen a more welcome sight.

Gaven drove up into the drive and didn't even get the motor stopped before the front screen door burst open. Two very excited little girls ran across the wide porch and pounded down the steps shouting, "Tessie, Tessie! You're home!"

Siegrid and Vega swarmed over her almost before she could crawl down out of the truck, and certainly before Gaven could come to assist her. She held them close to her, burying her face in their hair, and inhaling their clean, soft little-girl smells. How she'd missed them.

With more door slams, Mama was there and Edith right behind her, taking turns hugging her, offering the love, acceptance and welcome she hungered for. A bit slower, Pastor Stedman came hatless down the step, his thick hair and bushy mustache shining whiter than ever in the midday sun.

Now Gaven was by her side. "Mama, Edith, everyone," she said, "I want you to meet Gaven MacIntyre."

Tessa beamed as Mama stepped over and took Gaven's hands and gazed up at him. "Handsome she said you vere, Mr. MacIntyre. Wrote it in her letters she did," Mama said through her thick Swedish accent. "It wasn't the half she told us."

"Nor did she tell me she inherited all her charm and beauty from her mother, Mrs. Jurgen," Gaven said, returning the compliment. Mama blushed and the girls giggled.

"Aw pawsh, what's all this mister and missus business," Pastor said as he approached the little group. He reached out his large hand to Gaven. "I'm Royce Stedman, Gaven." He waved at Tessa's Mama. "And this here is Gerda, but I suppose you'll soon be calling her 'Mama.'" His eyes twinkled and he winked, but Gaven wasn't in the least embarrassed by the comment.

"Pastor, you're probably right!" Turning to Mama he said, "May I call you Gerda?"

"Gerda iss good. For now," she said winking just as Pastor had. Tessa was pleased to see her mother so happy and jovial. Such a change from last spring after Papa was murdered.

"And Edith here is my helpmate and mother of our four grown sons," Pastor continued. "She's cooked us up one scrumptious dinner. That table in there's so full, it's creaking and groaning."

"Oh Pastor," said five-year-old Vega, "the table's not groaning." Pastor looked shocked. "Vega Jurgen. Are you telling me you can't hear the table groaning? You probably forgot to wash your ears when you took your bath last Saturday night." He smoothed his mustache as he shook his head in disbelief. The girls continued giggling at his antics.

Tessa never thought she would ever see her family so happy. The joy and warmth surrounding her was almost too much to fathom. As they slowly made their way into the house, Pastor Stedman put his arm around Tessa's shoulders. "Welcome home, Peanut. You've not grown a smidgeon. Still a little bitty half pint."

"Oh she's grown all right," Gaven put in. "In ways not obvious to the eye."

Pastor paused to listen. Mama stopped at the front screen.

"When she walked through a crowd of trouble-makers at the Tulsa courthouse to visit two lonely, frightened boys in jail last spring, she was ten feet tall!"

"We heard a little bit about that story," Pastor said. "Now you can fill us in on every detail."

"Ya," Mama said, looking at Tessa with admiration shining in her eyes. "Every detail ve vant to hear."

Pastor guided Gaven into the parlor to sit and talk while dinner was dished up and served. Tessa had to agree with Pastor—the table was groaning under the load. And it was all for her. They wanted to impress her Gaven, and they had done a splendid job.

Dinner was a relaxed, enjoyable time of much talking, laughing, and merriment. They did talk of the riot, for they had received few details in the Glenn Pool. Pastor was pleased that Gaven and Tessa were continuing to assist, and pleased he could have a small part in the work. It was through him that Tessa and Gaven coordinated the purchase of supplies at the lumberyard.

At one point in the conversation, Gaven said to Mama, "Would it please you to know your daughter may be enrolling at Tulsa University at mid-semester?"

Mama hands flew to her rosy cheeks. "My little Tessa? At a uniwersity? Mercy gracious!"

"...versity, Mama," nine-year-old Siegrid corrected. "The word is university." She gave Tessa an exasperated look. "I'm trying my best!"

"You're doing well," Tessa complimented her. "What do you think, Mama?"

"But money. So much money. You earn that much?" She covered her mouth. "Sorry to ask that," she apologized as Pastor and Edith chuckled.

"She may qualify for a scholarship," Gaven told them.

Tessa laid her hand on Gaven's arm. "Gaven knows a professor who wants to help me."

Pastor picked up the towel-lined bowl full of golden yeast rolls and handed them to Gaven. "Have another one," he offered, then said, "Tessa's smart enough for any test they give her. She'll be the best student that university ever produced! Mark my word."

Pastor's comments while flattering were a surprise to Tessa since she knew he was not a man of idle words. Perhaps she did have a chance at that degree after all.

"And I agree." Gaven took two rolls and passed the bowl on. "And speaking of Tessa, I wanted to take this opportunity to formally ask you who love her the most, for her hand in marriage." He took Tessa's hand as he said it. Tessa gave a little gasp. She had no idea he'd planned this.

"Well, now, I don't know," Pastor said slowly. "You know Gerda here, she's pretty fussy about her kids. What do you think, Gerda? Does he measure up?"

"Fussy I am at that," Mama said to Gaven. "But you would win over the best of the fussy."

Pastor boomed out his deep laugh. "I can't top that comment. Edith, what do you think?"

"I think Gerda's right. I think Tessa's found God's choice for her life's companion."

Before Gaven could answer, Vega jumped down from her place and came up behind where Gaven and Tessa were sitting. She put her arms around them both. "I want you to get married! You have my permission." Which set them all to laughing.

After dinner, the girls showed Tessa to their room, which was the room where Tessa stayed when she lived there. The roomy upstairs bedrooms once accommodated all of the Stedman sons who were now married and gone. Edith loved having someone to fill those empty rooms.

The girls were excited about the big bed they slept in, and the new dresses hanging in the closet. In a few weeks they would begin attending the one-room school where Tessa had taught.

"How long do you think you'll be living here?" Tessa asked the girls as she admired the bright gingham dresses which Mama and Edith had lovingly stitched. "Will it be long?"

"Mama says we should get a place of our own," Siegrid said toying with one of her long blonde pigtails. As the older of the two, she was more serious than peppy, vivacious Vega. "Aunt Edith says there's no reason to get another place when she has all this room. But Mama wants to at least pay rent."

Vega bounced up and down on the edge of the big bed making her golden curls bounce. "Pastor told me we would live here forever and ever. He said not even handsome husbands could take us away from him." She giggled and fell over backward. "I want to live here forever. I love my soft, soft bed."

Later, they all sat around talking in the parlor while the girls took turns looking at pictures in the stereoscope. Since Edith had a shoe box full of the stereograph pictures, the girls were kept busy for hours, letting out a little gasp now and then as they viewed a particularly amazing scene from a faraway land.

The air was still and heavy in the room. No electricity here to run an oscillating fan to at least keep the air moving. But Tessa didn't care. In spite of the heat, she wished their stay could be longer.

At one point, the conversation turned to Hod Latham. Gaven definitely wanted to know more about this strange man who'd "won" Tessa in a deal with Tessa's father.

"He's one of those who's making money off prohibition," Pastor said. "His moonshine used to be brewed up for a few locals, but that's all changed now. The drier other parts of the country become, the more he's in demand. I understand he's in cahoots with a bunch from Arkansas now."

"At least we feel he's too busy to think about Tessa anymore," Edith added in her soft voice.

"Who could know what Aldan was thinking of?" Mama said, referring to the girls' father. "Whiskey poisons the mind."

"Is your father buried near here?" Gaven asked Tessa.

She pointed toward the church. "There in the churchyard cemetery."

"Can we... Would you want to walk over there?"

Vega jumped up. "Let's all go! Let's all go and take a walk."

Pastor reached out and scooped Vega up in air as she let out a squeal. "Sorry Little Bit, but I think this is a private thing for two lovebirds. Let's you and I go chip ice for the lemonade."

Chapter 6

Insects whirred in the tall grass, and long-legged grasshoppers leaped from the path as Tessa and Gaven walked hand-in-hand past the front steps of little church over to the graveyard.

"Everyone likes you." Tessa stepped back out of the way as Gaven lifted the wire loop and opened the fence gate to let her inside. The hinges creaked in protest as he closed it.

"I like them, too. Pastor Stedman is a gentle soul. But then I knew he would be from all you've told me. And I love to listen to your mama talk—reminds me of my father's heavy brogue." Gaven's straw hat was pushed back and his unruly chestnut hair fell in a tangled mass across his forehead. He was in his shirtsleeves with the cuffs rolled back, the fine hairs on his arms glistening in the hot afternoon sun. "I wish my folks were here so I could show you off to them. I've written them, but it's just not the same."

"You told me they used to live in Oklahoma. Why'd they leave?"

"Mother never did think much of the place to begin with. It was Dad and my older brother, Montgomery—Monty we call him, who talked her into coming. There wasn't enough action in Pennsylvania oil to suit them. They wanted a piece of what was happening in Tulsa. I was only about twelve when we came. Monty was almost eighteen."

"What happened?"

"I'm not sure. I guess Dad wasn't enough of a wheeler-dealer. He finally wound up working out on the rigs and Mother hated that. She's British and I think Tulsa was a little too rowdy for her liking."

Tessa led him up the curving dirt tracks through the stands of cedar and scrub oaks toward the back section of the cemetery.

"Monty was able to get in on the bigger stuff, and finally moved to Texas to work with an outfit there," he went on. "When I left for France, that was when Mother insisted on returning to her beloved Pennsylvania. Poor Dad finally gave in."

Tessa pointed to the plain white headstone. "There. That's it."

Gaven released her hand and knelt down, reading aloud. "'Aldan Jurgen, born 1881, died 1921.' Was he Swedish?"

Tessa shook her head. "German."

Gaven nodded. "Not much of an epitaph." He looked up at her, squinting against the sun.

"What could we say? Mama said since she didn't talk bad about him when he was alive, she wouldn't talk bad about him after he was gone. But she wouldn't lie either and say nice words when there were no nice words to say."

"I can hear your mama saying that. Makes sense." He reached up to her then and pulled her down beside him where they sat for a while beside the grave.

"Where's Berg buried?" Gaven wanted to know.

"Just a short way from our old cabin, back in the Sasakwa Hills where he loved to go hunting. I wish he were buried here." She paused, flicking a ladybug from her skirt. "But I guess it doesn't matter since he's really in heaven anyway."

Gaven touched her face gently. "Your father may have been a cruel man, Tessa, but you've risen above that."

"I hope so," she said. Knowing Hod Latham was still on the loose didn't make her any too sure.

"When you became a Christian, the scripture says you became a new creature. Being new in Him can make the past all clean."

He was right. And it was a lovely thought. But before she could ponder it further, he had pulled her to him, smothering her face in warm sweet kisses, finally placing one gently on her waiting lips. "Never forget that I love you with all my heart," he whispered.

Later, as they walked back to the house, Tessa wrestled with the question of what Gaven's proper British mother might think of a girl whose father was killed in a bootlegging quarrel? She might be a new creature like Gaven said, but would his mother think so?

Saying good-bye to her family was no longer an agonizing ordeal for Tessa. Seeing them safe and happy made it easier. Plus the fact that she and Gaven might be making a number of such trips as long as they were needed to get the lumber back to Tulsa.

Driving home was a great deal slower since the truck was loaded down with a heavy cargo. By the time they returned to Greenwood it was nearly dark. An excited group met them as they pulled up at Chloe's partially burned-out house. Chloe and Willard lived in a large tent pitched on the property and worked every spare hour to salvage what they could from the burned house, as well as helping others do the same.

Chloe was as gracious a hostess in her tent as she had been in her neat little two-story frame house. She made sure Tessa was comfortable while the men unloaded the lumber. And she was dying to know every detail of the visit.

"They loved Gaven," Tessa told her as they ate cornbread together at their makeshift table.

"Hey, what's there not to love? Course they all love that man."

"And while we were eating he formally asked all of them for my hand in marriage. Can you imagine such a thing?"

"My stars," she chuckled. "What a gentlemen he is. You so blessed, child."

"He wanted to see Papa's grave." Tessa took a drink from a glass of tepid tea.

"What he say about your no-count daddy?"

"He said I've risen above all that. He reminded me I'm a new creature in Jesus."

"He say that right. Now tell me, did you lay eyes on that Hod fellow?"

Tessa shook her head. "Like I told you the other night, he's too busy making bigger bootlegging deals. Pastor says he's doing business all the way over to the Arkansas line."

Chloe's brows raised. "Crossin' the state line? Sounds to me like that little man is getting too big for his britches."

"He must be raking in a bundle of money."

"Figure that out," Chloe said. "The Klan say they don't want nothing to do with the wets. They say they all for prohibition, but the likes of Hod Latham can pay his ten-dollar dues and be a member. Don't make no sense to me."

"We've not heard much from the Klan since the riot. Have they backed off?"

"Maybe they washed they hands of us for a time. They did about all the damage they can do here. But Willard done heard they was burning crosses on the hills outside of Oklahoma City last week. They quiet, but not too quiet."

Tessa jumped at the sound of Gaven's voice calling to her from outside the tent. "Tessa, we're all unloaded."

"Thanks for the supper, Chloe." She gave her friend a hug.

"Thanks be to you and Gaven for helping bring in the supplies. We'll rebuild Greenwood yet!"

Later, as Gaven drove Tessa home, walked her to the Walsh's front porch, and kissed her good-night, Tessa felt the day had been very nearly perfect. Before she could go to bed, she had yet to share the details with Mina and Pauline who were waiting up for her. But she didn't mind. She wanted to shout it to the whole world how incredible her Gaven truly was, and how blessed she was to have him.

GAVEN SET UP A TIME for Tessa to meet with Dr. Edward Misek at his office at the university. Now that September had arrived, Gaven returned to teaching and his evenings were free. "I'll pick you up after work and drive you out," he told her when the appointment was first arranged.

Throughout that day, Tessa could hardly keep her mind on yardage, fabrics, spools, or prices. What if she said something wrong? What if the professor had heard the gossip about her involvement with the rebuilding of Greenwood? What if she didn't qualify for a scholarship? Round and round went the spinning thoughts like the carousel at the park. One moment she was agonizing, the next moment she told herself that a degree didn't matter all that much anyway.

Even Floy noticed her distracted state when she came to relieve Tessa at lunch. Glancing up at the bolts on the shelves, she said, "Tessa, what's the Canton crepe doing over with the chiffon taffeta?"

"Oh my." Tessa hurried over to pull it out and shove it into the correct place. "I sure don't want Ila to see that. I'd be in even more hot water. While I'm at lunch, if you have no customers, would you take a minute and double check my math on the morning's sales tickets? I may have overlooked something."

Floy leaned on the counter popping her gum. "You sure are acting edgy. What's up?"

"I wish it didn't show. I'm a mess of nerves. Gaven is taking me to meet one of his English professors at the college."

"You mean the *university*? The name's changed, you know."

"Yes, of course, I mean the university. I've never been so nervous. Even when I took the county exam to start teaching I wasn't this nervous."

"What's so important about meeting a stuffy old professor?"

"Gaven feels this professor can advise me about applying for a scholarship."

"You want to *attend* there?" Floy's eyes grew wide.

"Mm hm." She'd not shared her little secret with Floy before. There'd been no reason to.

"But I thought you were getting married."

"I am."

Jamming her hands into the pockets of her smock, Floy said, "That doesn't make any sense at all. If you're gonna have Gaven to take care of you, why go to school? What a bore. What a drudge."

"Not for me. I want to learn." She patted her midsection. "There's something deep down inside me that hungers for more learning."

"Whew," Floy countered with a laugh. "I guess I can be thankful there isn't anything like that crawling around on the inside of me."

"I know it sounds a little silly, but it's the only way I know how to describe how I feel. It's a longing, a yearning."

"The only longing and yearning I have is for a nice husband. And I hope he comes along soon. Oops, there comes Ila. You'd better scoot on to lunch."

"You'll look over the sales slips?"

"Sure, sure. With the dither you're in, you'll need someone following along behind you today."

Chapter 7

Although the evenings were hot for September, the drive out Eleventh Street was pleasant as the breeze blew in through the windows of the roadster.

"You're awfully quiet," Gaven commented. "Almost as quiet as you were when I first met you."

"I'll probably never be that quiet again," she answered remembering how tongue-tied she used to be whenever she was with him. "Right now I'm so nervous I can hardly breathe."

"This means a great deal to you, doesn't it?"

"I need to be back in the classroom, and unless I return to a country school, this is the only way."

"But you'd never be satisfied with that again would you?"

She shook her head. "Not after seeing the classrooms at Riverview."

"I thought not."

The three-story Kendall Hall loomed even larger than it did the first time she saw the campus. Gazing up at the large bell tower, she wondered if she had what it took to break into that formidable-looking fortress?

Their shoes squeaked on the polished parquet floors in the long hallway as Gaven guided her to the professor's office. The door was open. The outer office was empty, so Gaven tapped on the door frame. "Anyone here?"

"That you Gaven?" Dr. Misek appeared at the door of his office. "Please excuse me. My secretary's gone home. Come on in." The tall man's rumpled suit bagged on his lithe frame. "Good to see you Gaven." He pointed them to two chairs near his desk. "And this is..."

"Professor, this is my fiancé, Tessa Jurgen."

Tessa accepted his warm handshake.

"Thank you for staying late to meet with us, Dr. Misek," Gaven said.

"Think nothing of it. I rarely get away before this time of day anyway."

Dr. Misek's thin graying hair was combed with a center part, and the round wire-rimmed glasses gave his narrow face a pinched look. If Floy were to see his stiff collar, she'd sure enough say he was "stuffy." But Tessa was enchanted not only with Dr. Misek, but also with his office full of books and papers. Tall double-hung windows situated above a row of wooden file cabinets, were wide open letting in the evening breeze.

"Gaven tells me you're interested in becoming a student here at the university," the professor began. "I understand you've already had experience teaching."

"With a county certificate." Her throat felt too dry to talk; nervousness had turned her mouth to cotton.

"She taught at a small school near the Glenn Pool." Gaven jumped in to save her. "Mostly children of some of the oil field hands and the roustabouts. No easy job."

Dr. Misek rolled his chair up to his desk. Sitting straight he touched his fingertips together. "Let's let Miss Jurgen speak for herself."

"Gaven, could you get me a cup of water?" Tessa asked.

He jumped up. "There's a water cooler in the hall. I'll be back in a moment.

"I'm sorry, Dr. Misek. I'm a little nervous. I've never met a college professor before."

"I see." Now Dr. Misek gave a hint of a smile. "Suppose you tell me about your schooling."

"I grew up in the Sasakwa Hills and attended a country school there through eighth grade. Then..."

"Here's the water," Gaven said, handing her a small paper cup. She thanked him and tipped up the cup letting the wetness soothe away the parched feeling.

"And then...?" the professor said.

"Oh yes, then I attended a year of high school, but when the opportunity came to take the county exam I jumped at the chance."

"She passed with flying colors, too," Gaven added.

"We'll get the scores from the county superintendent's office," the professor said again with a slight smile. "'Flying colors' may look different on paper. And then you did private teaching, is that right?"

"I taught for the Patton family."

"The children of Henry Patton?" Now the professor dipped his pen in the inkwell and scribbled a few notes on a pad.

"Only the two younger children. The older daughter was at boarding school when I began last January."

"You're still there?"

Tessa drank the rest of the water. "I'm not employed by the Pattons now. I work at Halliburton-Abbott department store. In dry goods."

"And the reason for leaving?" The long pen was poised.

Tessa glanced at Gaven. Would the truth make her lose her chance?

Gaven leaned forward a bit. "Sir, you know the Pattons, I'm sure."

"I do."

"If I might say so, money sometimes makes people become a little fickle."

"Are you telling me Mrs. Henry Patton became fickle about the governess of her children?"

Gaven cleared his throat. "You could say that."

"I can believe it. Now then, I thought you told me the two of you are engaged."

"We are," Tessa said quickly. "We plan to be married in January, right after Christmas."

The professor leveled a gaze at Gaven. "You want your wife going to school?"

"Very much, sir."

The professor straightened his glasses then drummed the pen. "All right. That's good. Just as long as you both are in agreement. Very important that you agree." He dipped the pen again. "I'll send for your records tomorrow. Meanwhile, I'll set up a time for you to come in and take your entrance examination. At that time, we'll also have you apply for available scholarships. The tests will take most of the day."

"Then make it on Thursday. That's my day off."

"A week from Thursday." He took a small card and filled out the time and date and handed it to Tessa.

As they stood to go, Gaven asked, "Do you think she has a chance at a scholarship, sir?"

"Well now, Mr. MacIntyre, I know you think I'm a genius, but I'm not able to look into this girl's head and read what she has there. I suggest we just wait and see. Fair enough?"

"Forgive me for being presumptuous." Gaven reached out to shake hands with the professor. "Thank you for your time."

"You're most welcome." To Tessa he said, "You can report here to my office that morning and I'll show you were to go to take the tests."

Thanking him once again, Tessa and Gaven grabbed hands excitedly and hurried back to the car. As Tessa looked at the card in her hand, an involuntary shiver swept over her. She was one step closer.

———— ⊙ ————

TESSA HAD WANTED TO go to the monthly City Council meeting right alongside Chloe and Willard, but Gaven thought better of it. "No sense in provoking any more hostilities," he said. And in the end even Miles advised against it.

"Not that we wouldn't want your company," Chloe told her, "but you and Gaven go on and sit on the white side and just be praying."

Now as Tessa surveyed the packed courtroom, she could see they were right. The city council ordinarily met in city hall, but interest in city matters had grown so since the riot, the mayor had it move to the courthouse two blocks over on Boulder. The largest first-floor courtroom was needed to hold the spectators. As usual, the blacks occupied one half, the whites the other. At the front of the room sitting at a long table, were the mayor and the five council members.

Beside her, Gaven sat stiffly with his hat in his lap. Beads of sweat formed on his smooth upper lip, and he was no doubt wishing he'd come in his shirtsleeves as a few others had. The oppressive heat blanketed the room. The air was alive with the fluttering of many hand-held fans. Chloe was sitting almost directly across the aisle from Tessa so that periodically they caught one another's eye and gave a smile—or a certain look.

Earlier in the summer, Miles and Lanny had been successful in thwarting the efforts on behalf of the mayor's office to completely relocate the black community further to the outskirts of the city. Quickly following on the heels of that, motions were heard to construct a new railroad station on the site of the Greenwood community. When that fell down defeated, a new fire ordinance was proposed. That too was defeated. But meanwhile, as the months dragged on, the need for shelter for the citizens of Greenwood was virtually ignored.

Presently, the mayor called the City Council meeting to order with a grave warning that the least little disturbance would result in that person being expelled from the room and the meeting being adjourned to a smaller room with no spectators.

True to form, the commissioners left the business of the problems of Greenwood until the very last thing on the agenda. Children were restless, babies were crying, and the spectators were fidgeting before the issue came to the table to be discussed. At last, Miles was granted time to speak.

With his talent and ability of clear articulation, he presented the needs for building permits. "To date, according to City Hall records, over five hundred permits have been filed. Of these, only thirty-five have been processed and approved."

"If you will recall," one commissioner retorted, "these applications hit the workers in city hall in a flood. We have no staff adequate to process them quickly. And don't forget, none could be processed until the matter of the fire ordinance had been resolved."

"Yes, that's true," Miles agreed, his voice clear and calm. "But now that all other matters have been resolved, it would seem a reasonable request that emergency measures might be considered to expedite the process. Houses will be needed for these displaced families before winter comes. Especially families with small children."

From behind her, Tessa heard a loud whisper, "They shoulda thought of that before they started the uprising!"

Tessa moved to look to see who was speaking, but Gaven reached over to take her by the hand, giving her a sidelong glance as he did. His glance told her to, "Sit still and stay quiet."

Discussion went back and forth among council members, and mayor and various citizens, continually coming up with the same conclusion—that the offices at city hall were doing their best, but were terribly understaffed for such an undertaking.

Suddenly Tessa was on her feet. "Mr. Mayor, might I address the council?"

Fans stopped moving as Tessa felt all eyes riveted on her.

How could she have stood so quickly? She dared not look to either side.

"Your name please?" the mayor said.

She swallowed hoping her dry throat would allow her to speak. "Tessa Jurgen."

"*Miss* Jurgen?"

"Yes sir."

The secretary was furiously writing in her shorthand notebook.

"What would you like to say to the council, Miss Jurgen?"

"It seems to me the problem here lies only in lack of manpower. But volunteers from around the city are already in place at various churches working on distributing the supplies." She paused a moment, then felt Gaven reach up to slip his hand into hers. "Why couldn't some of this paperwork also be given to volunteers? Surely a place in city hall could be designated as a center where volunteers might come in and be put to work."

"Any comments from the commissioners?" the mayor asked.

"Yes sir," spoke up the Street Commissioner. "Miss Jurgen here seems to think the processing of legal documents can be compared to sorting clothing and tableware. A noble idea, Mr. Mayor, but horribly impractical."

As Tessa sat down, whispers around her buzzed like angry insects. Gaven tightened his grip on her hand. He looked over at her and smiled. She thought he might be upset with her for drawing attention to them, but his smile said otherwise.

Just then, a lady two rows in front of Tessa stood up. "Mr. Mayor, I happen to be a volunteer in the relief effort. I am also a graduate of the University of Kansas and I can type. I believe Miss Jurgen raises a valid point. There are several of us who can sort clothes, but we are also capable of doing *more* than sorting clothes. There shouldn't be anything too hard about filling out permits. If this were undertaken, I'd be pleased to head up the volunteer group."

Tessa stole a look at Chloe who was fairly beaming.

"That won't be necessary," came a loud voice from the back.

Tessa turned about in the hard seat to see Trevalene Patton standing there dressed to the hilt in a crimson hat with draping veil and matching silk dress.

"I was on the coast for most of the summer," she continued, "but now that I've returned I'm working very hard to pick up the pieces of all the relief efforts and to coordinate them so they flow more smoothly. Since the volunteer work being discussed would come under the same jurisdiction, I don't believe we'll need anyone to oversee any volunteer group. That will be my job."

The other lady started to reply, but the mayor interrupted her. "Mrs. Patton, the city of Tulsa certainly owes you our deep appreciation for all your hard work. However, with all due respect, since there's been no decision as yet, there's no need to decide who should head up the group."

"Be that as it may," Trevalene retorted in her heavy southern drawl, "my point is, if and when that group ever comes into being, I *will* be head over it."

Clearing his throat the mayor profusely thanked her again. "Now I'll be grateful if you ladies will please take your seats so the meeting may continue."

There were no more comments from the commissioners. Someone moved that the meeting be adjourned. Again, Miles was on his feet. "Sir, may we be given a date by which we can expect the permits to begin being processed and dispersed?"

A commissioner said, "There's no reason to give a date—the permits are even now being processed."

Tessa looked at Chloe who rolled her eyes. They'd heard that statement ever since the riot occurred in June.

"Well then," Miles pressed in carefully, "may we be given an approximate date for the completion of the processing?

Several of the commissioners laughed. "That would be highly unlikely," the mayor replied, "since we don't even know if we have all the applications in yet. Don't forget, you're not the only people in Tulsa who are building right now. We have the normal flow of permits from citizens other than the group you're representing."

Miles sat down then. There was no more business. The meeting was adjourned.

Slowly the stuffy courtroom was emptied of its occupants. Gently Gaven guided Tessa through the crowd. Arm-in-arm they walked through the foyer to the front door. A few people along the way commented favorably to Tessa regarding her idea. Tessa felt that most of the citizens truly wanted to help Greenwood rebuild, but the handful who did not were the ones with the most power, the most money, and the loudest voices.

She breathed deeply of the cool night air as they emerged from the building. There at the foot of the steps stood Trevalene and Henry Patton as though waiting for them. Tessa felt Gaven stiffen. Had Trevalene been a few pounds lighter, and had her eyes been softer, she would have looked like a fashion plate standing there dressed in her cranberry silk, which shimmered beneath the glowing streetlight.

The crowd thinned quickly, so if Trevalene was looking for an audience she didn't quite achieve it. In a rather loud voice she said, "My dear *little* Miss Jurgen, how conscientious of you to make such a good suggestion to the council. How I wish I'd thought of it myself. But then, I have been rather busy."

"Come Trevalene." Henry placed his bowler hat on his head and reached out to take his wife's arm, but she pulled from his grip.

"It was especially good of you since you were the very one who caused those poor nigras so much heartache."

Gaven's roadster was parked down the street just past where the Pattons were standing. Just as he'd done in the church that day, Gaven steered her away from the path of the accusations. In a low whisper, he said, "Lovely night for a walk *around* the block, don't you think, Miss Jurgen."

"Lovely, Mr. MacIntyre," she replied.

Chapter 8

G aven drove around the city for a time before they went to Chloe's tent, just in case they were being followed. Those who had gathered to discuss the meeting were divided in their reactions. Some felt the showing of so many of their number was a positive thing. That it proved they were not going to quit until Greenwood was totally rebuilt. Others were more cautious saying they felt it only made the belligerent leaders more belligerent.

They were sitting around an open fire in what was once Chloe and Willard's front yard. The coffee pot was on and bubbling, permeating the night air with its rich aroma.

"I likes that lady who stood up and say she have a degree," Willard said as he took a brimming tin cup that Chloe offered him. He blew on the steaming dark liquid before taking a sip. "Shows me not ever'body want to see us go down."

Chloe smiled. "Well, I likes the spunky little gal what brought up the good idea in the first place."

Gaven put his arm around Tessa's shoulder and pulled her to him. "Me too!" he said.

The meeting lasted long into the night as they laid plans. The most they could hope to do, Miles advised, was to cooperate with city hall as much as possible. "Every time we get a permit, we'll have a house-raisin' party," he joked.

"That means we'll just have parties all winter long," his partner added.

But Tessa knew it wasn't that simple. Nor was it any kind of joke. Winter was right around the corner.

THE NEXT MORNING EARLY, Tessa was hurrying to keep up with Floy as they tripped up the stairs to the fourth-floor employee lounge area. Before store hours, employees had to take the stairs rather than the elevators since the operators had not yet arrived.

"What's this meeting about?" Tessa paused at one of the landings to catch her breath before they went on.

"Search me. Something about Mr. Osborn wanting the store clerks to learn more about other departments. I think he wants us to become more interchangeable. In case of sickness and stuff like that." The popping of Floy's gum echoed in the enclosed stairwell.

Boyd Osborn, manager of Halliburton-Abbott, was forever coming up with new ideas for higher efficiency in his store. While Tessa had utmost respect for the man, this sounded like one of his better ideas.

"I'd be thankful for a few days away from heavy bolts of fabric," Tessa said as she pushed open the heavy door on third floor.

Floy lowered her voice as they approached the lounge which was filling up with the other clerks. "And I'd love to play around in millinery and get away from the pots and pans," she whispered. "I just love hats!"

The rumor which Floy had heard turned out to be correct. Come Monday morning there would be a systematic switching of store personnel. Mr. Osborn presented the announcement with all the flair of a grand opening. Floy once told Tessa that Mr. Osborn had all his suits tailor-made, never buying one in his own men's department. Whether or not it was true, the manager was always impeccably dressed with his brown-blond hair shiny with brilliantine, and not a hair out of place.

"The schedules are now being carefully formulated by my secretary." Mr. Osborn flashed his toothpaste-ad smile to the small group. "The rotations will progress slowly and, we believe, efficiently. By the new year, we hope that every clerk will have the ability, with no problems, to perform in at least two and perhaps three stations in the store."

After a few questions and even fewer comments, the meeting was concluded. Later that same day, Tessa learned she would be one of the first to be rotated. When Tessa returned from her lunch break, Floy had the news. Floy always seemed to know the scuttlebutt.

"Lucky you," she said, pressing at her unruly curls with her fingertips. "How can you be so lucky? You start Monday morning in accessories."

"Accessories? Are you sure?"

"I'm sure. I saw the list myself."

"What a nice change from smelly fabrics to soft kid gloves and lace hankies."

"And the jewelry. Don't forget the jewelry." Floy rolled her dark eyes. "And I'll still be pushing around the pots and pans. What do you bet when I am moved, I'll probably have to stay here with your heavy bolts of cloth."

Tessa chuckled at her friend's pessimism. "They're not *my* bolts, Floy. But I tell you what—if you are rotated here, I'll gladly give them all to you!"

"What a friend." With a shake of her curly head, Floy returned to her housewares.

When Gaven picked her up after work, Tessa was pleased to tell him her good news. He too was thankful that she'd have a rest from the heavy bolts of cloth for a week or so. "That arm of yours needs a rest," he commented, and she agreed. It had been bothering her more than she wanted to admit.

Gaven was invited to have supper at the Walsh's and then he and Tessa planned to spend the evening studying. The back of the roadster was littered with his college textbooks.

Supper was a friendly happy affair, with Russ teasing and joking, and Mina placing never-ending bowls of enticing foods before them.

"I'll never be able to breathe again," Gaven said as he refused a third helping of the roast beef. "And we're going to try to study tonight." He looked at Tessa. "I'll have to drink ten cups of coffee just to keep my eyes open."

"You know where the coffee pot is," Pauline said as she rose to help clear the table. "Help yourself."

"I think I hear Tin Lizzie calling me." Russ pushed himself back from the table. "I swear I spend as much time fixing her as I do driving her."

After the dishes were done, with Gaven cheerfully lending a hand, Pauline and Mina retired to the sewing room. Tessa had brought home several nice pieces of fabric from the remnant table and they were planning to cut out and sew new blouses.

Gaven brought the books into the parlor and there they spread them out and settled in. Gaven felt history, grammar and mathematics would be the most important areas. He skimmed through the materials, grilling her as he went. By the time he was ready to leave, Gaven said he was bushed, even though he did down two cups of coffee. Tessa, on the other hand, was stimulated. It seemed the more she learned, the more she wanted to learn, as though it were an endless thirst.

"May I keep the books here for a few days? I can study in the evenings on my own."

"Well, of course. They just sit in my bookshelves at the boarding house, taking up space." Just as Gaven stood to leave, Russ stuck his head in the door.

"You two about finished? What do you say we churn up a freezer of ice cream."

Gaven shook his head. "Thanks Russ, but I still have papers to grade before I turn in."

"You didn't tell me you had more work to do," Tessa chided him. "You should have brought it with you. I could have helped."

"I know. But your test day is coming fast, and I felt that was more important."

A flood of adoration rose up inside Tessa as she warmly thanked him for his unselfishness. Her love for him seemed to be exploding in growth spurts with each passing day.

As they walked together to Gaven's car, they could hear Russ on the back porch hammering at a block of ice in the gunny sack. He already had Mina in the kitchen mixing up the custard.

Someday her Gaven would be on their back porch chipping ice from the block and she would be in her very own kitchen fixing custard for the ice cream freezer. What a joyous happy day that would be. She could hardly wait.

———— ◉ ————

AN EXCITED TESSA ARRIVED at work in the accessories department the next Monday morning. How different from dry goods. The cases here were filled with exquisite fur necklaces, some of fox, some mink and the most expensive were of ermine. Boxes and boxes of the sheerest silk stockings lined the shelves; broaches, long beaded necklaces, and gold engraved pendant watches lay glittering in the jewelry cases.

A congenial, matronly lady named Agnes Hulse had worked in accessories for many years. She didn't at all resent Tessa's coming in to learn. Agnes taught Tessa the colors, brands and textures of the hosiery, as well as the sizes and types of gloves. Time flew as she studied the boxes of lace handkerchiefs, and prices of jewelry. By afternoon, she'd made several sales and yet felt none of the fatigue she'd experienced in the dry goods department.

"You learn quickly, my dear," Agnes said as she tucked a pencil into her graying bun. "I never did think you belonged in dry goods."

Actually, Tessa didn't feel she belonged in a department store at all, but after the first day, she was convinced accessories was a far sight better than dry goods.

The next afternoon, Agnes was out to lunch and Tessa was studying the boxes of hosiery. Agnes had asked that she check to see every box was in its correct place. As she did, she tried to memorize the brands, sizes, and colors.

A rapping sounded on the counter behind her as a customer said, "Miss, I'm looking for a pair of long gloves to wear to an evening dance."

"Yes, right over here," Tessa said turning around. Then she froze. There at her counter stood Sadella Patton.

The Patton's older daughter was a long-legged, gangly young girl with eyes as cold as her mother's. Standing a full head taller than Tessa, she now looked down at her with detached disdain.

"Well if it isn't little Miss Jurgen," she said mimicking her mother's emphasis on the word *little*. She glanced around the accessories department. "Working in an old department store? Quite a change from the Patton mansion."

"The gloves are in this case," Tessa said making her way to another counter away from Sadella. Sliding open the case door, she said, "Long gloves you said? Any particular color?"

"Shelby's taking me to a ball at the Sinclair's," she announced.

Tessa pulled out several boxes of elbow-length gloves, some of kid, others of silk with tiny pearl buttons at the wrist placket. "What shade is your dress?"

"Eggshell. Mother and I picked it up in New York last week."

"Here are two in eggshell. Would you care to try on a pair?"

"Know why we were in New York, little Miss Tessa?"

Of course, Tessa cared nothing about why Sadella and Trevalene were in New York. Spending money was usually the main objective. Sadella picked up one of the silk gloves and began to work it on her thin hand, but her fingers were too long for that size. Obviously miffed, she yanked it off. "Give me something in my size," she demanded.

Obediently, Tessa pulled out a larger size. If this spoiled child were to make a scene, it could look very bad for Tessa. Thankfully, this glove fit. "You never answered me," she said holding up her hand to admire the glove, running her other hand over the silkiness. "Want to know why Mother and I were in New York?" she asked again.

"Tell me, Sadella, why were you in New York?"

Slowly she drew on the other glove. "Mother and I were shopping for my wedding dress."

Tessa attempted to mask her shock.

"You're surprised, but you shouldn't be. Shel and I have been in love ever since we were little kids. Now that you and that silly New York reporter, Clarette what's-her-name, are out of my way, things happened rather quickly. Shel and I are announcing our engagement next week."

"Shall I ring up the gloves?" How could Shel do such a thing? Tessa wondered. He must be out of his mind, hooking himself up with such an empty girl. Tessa was sure of one thing—Shelby Harland had never been, and would never be, in love with Sadella Patton.

"He's taking me to Europe on our honeymoon. Probably Paris. I've been to Paris many times, but it's so much better when a person is in love." She put her hands to her face and Tessa feared she would smear some of her blood-red lip rouge on the gloves. "A spring wedding will be perfect for sailing off to Paris. There's nothing like springtime in Paris."

"I'm very happy for you, Miss Patton. Now if you'll just remove the gloves, I'll box them up for you. Will they go on the Patton account?"

Remembering how Sadella ruthlessly accused Jasper Franklin of attacking her, made Tessa's anger smolder deep inside. If the girl had not created her far-fetched story and made false accusations, Jasper might still be alive today. He would have been going off to college this fall.

"If the dance weren't this very Friday evening," Sadella went on, "I'd buy my gloves in New York instead of this rinky-dink little store. Macy's on Fifth Avenue is my very favorite."

Tessa busied herself putting the other gloves back in the case. Carrying the empty box for the gloves Sadella was wearing, she walked to the cash register and wrote up the sale. Sadella followed like a child.

"Is this to be on the Patton account, or will it be cash?"

"On the account of course." Sadella pulled off the gloves and handed them over. Tessa neatly folded them back into the tissue paper lining of the box and closed it up. "Please sign here." She pushed the sales pad across the counter.

"Shel's parents are thrilled about the wedding." Sadella scribbled her name on the slip. "And so are Mother and Daddy. Everyone's so happy for me." She pushed the pad back toward Tessa. "It'll be the social event of the entire year. There'll probably be an outdoor reception in the formal gardens."

Pulling string from the spool hanging from a holder above the counter, Tessa tied the box neatly. Taking the small scissors from the pocket of her smock, she snipped the string. "I hope you enjoy the gloves, Miss Patton."

Sadella picked up the box and turned to go, then turned back. "Too bad you had to get kicked out on your ear. Otherwise, you could have been there for all the gay festivities."

Tessa calmly turned back to straightening the hosiery boxes, ignoring the remark. But deep inside she was seething.

Chapter 9

Thursday morning Tessa took the trolley out to the university. That is, she rode it as far as it went, then she had to walk the rest of the way. University students, she understood, were petitioning city hall to have the trolley line extended all the way to the campus. Tessa could understand why.

Before breakfast, Pauline and Mina had surprised her with a new dress for the occasion. "You're always bringing home the cloth," Mina said as they presented her with the gift, "so we decided to make you a new dress with some of it."

Tessa hardly knew what to say. She'd never had many clothes to begin with, but what she did have was lost in the riot. The dress was made of a soft pink print with a V-neck and rolled collar. The bodice and cuffs were finished in dainty pleating.

She thanked them profusely, trying hard to hold back tears.

"Wear your hair down," Pauline suggested. "It'll look lovely on the pink."

"But this isn't a beauty contest." She turned to Mina for her motherly advice. "Won't my braids look more respectable?"

"I think Pauline's right. Your golden hair is an asset. Fastened back, it still gives a respectable appearance. Tell me when you're ready, and I'll let you pick out one of my hats."

"No need for that, Mina," Tessa protested. "My straw one will do fine."

"Take her up on it," Pauline said with a laugh. "She hardly ever loans out a hat!"

By the time Tessa was completely ready she felt like a million dollars. She surveyed her appearance in the mirror. Mina's broad-brimmed pink felt hat with the chic white trim was perfect. As she picked up her bag and gloves to leave, Gaven called. He wanted to let her know he was praying for her. "Don't forget to get a cup of water *before* you go in to see the professor," came his joke over the telephone line.

"I'll remember."

And when she arrived at Kendall hall, she did exactly that, stopping at the water cooler down the hall from Dr. Misek's office. She drank one cupful, then carried another along with her as she went in to see him. The five-block walk from the end of the trolley line, coupled with her nervousness left her throat dry as paper.

Dr. Misek's secretary ushered her into his office, where he greeted her warmly leaning over his desk to shake her hand. "So good to see you again, Miss Jurgen. My my, how fine you look. Please have a chair." After pulling a file from the nearby cabinet he sat down opposite her. He opened the folder and glanced about his desk. "Now where did I put those glasses?" Spotting them on the credenza, he chuckled. "Oh yes, here they are." Glasses on, he scanned the sheets before him. "We've received the information from the county superintendent and I must say your test scores are impressive. It doesn't appear you'll have any problems here today."

"Thank you, Dr. Misek. Gaven's been helping me study."

His eyes beneath the shaggy gray brows twinkled as he quipped, "I hope he didn't coach you too much in grammar. Might do more harm than good." He laughed at his attempt at humor. "Come now, Miss Jurgen. Let me escort you to the library."

Together they walked up the broad marble steps to the next floor and into the library. There he introduced Tessa to Mrs. Detwiler who was to administer the tests. The lady, who looked at her through dark, serious eyes, was all business and of few words. Her thick frizzled graying hair was loosely fastened in a knot at the nape of her neck.

Tessa found herself wishing Mrs. Detwiler would at least offer a smile of encouragement.

She was led to a large table near the windows where she made herself comfortable, removing her gloves and placing them atop her handbag. While the tests were tedious, they weren't as difficult as she had feared. Between each one, Mrs. Detwiler allowed her to take short breaks. For lunch, she'd planned to eat the sandwich tucked into her bag, but Dr. Misek surprised her by coming in and offering to buy her lunch at the cafeteria in Kemp Lodge.

While she ate her meatloaf with gravy, he chatted with her as though they were long-lost relatives. The objects of conversation were two of the professor's favorites, his school and his family. Tessa wasn't sure of which he was the fondest.

By day's end, the university wasn't nearly as foreboding. In fact, she felt very much at home. There was no doubt in her mind she did quite well on every test—even social studies which wasn't her favorite. With God's help, by January she'd be a full-time student. The thought made her heart race as she caught the trolley back home late that afternoon.

<hr>

EACH DAY IN OCTOBER was more brilliant and clear than the one before. Nights were cool, and every day the sky shone a sharp blue as though it had been scrubbed. Every few weeks, Tessa and Gaven brought up another load of lumber from the Glenn Pool and on each trip the trees along the way were more vivid in their gold and crimson autumn dress.

Gaven fit right in with Tessa's family. He spent hours with Pastor Stedman while Tessa, Edith and Mama worked in an upstairs bedroom on the beginning stages of the wedding dress.

Pauline had discovered the style in the *Ladies Home Companion* magazine, and showed it to Tessa who was smitten with it. Using three different patterns, Edith and Mama were sure they could copy it.

Siegrid and Vega were as excited about the prospect of traveling to Tulsa, as they were about the upcoming wedding itself.

Rebuilding in Greenwood was painstakingly slow. But with every house raising, they turned it into a celebration, thus even the smallest progress was noticed. The main street, which was Greenwood, was totally cleared now, and basements were cleared of the rubble. Two buildings were going up. It was still a long way from the dozens that had stood there previously, but it was a start. Spirits were high.

It took the first cold autumn rain to bring those spirits plummeting down. Overnight temperatures plunged as sodden gray clouds moved in.

Tessa looked out her bedroom window that morning, staring at the sheets of rain and wondering about Chloe and the others. She heard Mina downstairs bustling around in the kitchen. Soon they would all be leaving for church. Mina's Sunday morning specialty was waffles with maple syrup and Tessa could almost taste them. She hurried about getting ready so she could go down and lend a hand.

Even Russ was a little subdued by the weather. "We need the rain," he mumbled as he loaded his steaming waffles with butter. "But I don't know why it has to get so cold so soon."

"It's fall Russell," Mina told him in her usual cheery voice. "It's supposed to get cold in the fall."

Before they returned thanks, Tessa asked if they could include a prayer for those living in the tents in Greenwood.

Russ nodded. "It's gonna be a rough winter over there," he said. His prayer was gracious and full of love and concern. Although Russell Walsh loved to tease and joke, he had a tender heart.

Since Gaven served as Sunday school superintendent, he arrived at church earlier than everyone else, so Tessa rode with the Walshes in their Model T.

When it was time to go, Russ pulled the rumbling automobile as near to the back door as possible, then held the large black umbrella for each of them as they skirted puddles from the back porch to the waiting car.

Teaching Sunday school, to some degree, appeased Tessa's need to teach. She adored the children in her first-grade class, but even they seemed a little grumpy on that dreary gray morning. She finally put away that morning's lesson and led them in a lively Bible quiz.

Gaven came to the door of her classroom when the Sunday School hour was over. Together they walked upstairs to the sanctuary.

"I can't get my mind off Chloe this morning," she told Gaven as they sat down in their pew.

"I knew you'd be thinking of them. I have been, too."

"When I heard that north wind blowing in the middle of the night, it made my heart ache. This is a winter I wish would never come."

"Shall we drive over there after church?"

Normally they had Sunday dinner with the Walshes, and were expected today as usual. "Let's do. I just want to be sure they're all right."

"I'll explain to Russ and Mina," Gaven said. "They'll understand."

As Tessa studied the tall glowing stained-glass window above the choir loft of the large sanctuary her thoughts turned to their upcoming wedding. She was glad Gaven agreed with her that their wedding should be held in the smaller chapel of the church rather than this cavernous sanctuary.

At first, she wanted the ceremony held at the Stedman's little country church where she'd first accepted Jesus as Lord of her life. But she had so many new friends in Tulsa, it would be quite impractical. So Pastor and Edith would come to them. It was Gaven who suggested they invite pastor to perform the ceremony. Once again, Tessa was deeply touched by her fiancé's sensitivity. At times she felt she would burst from the joy of it all. Just his physical presence beside her gave her a sense of reassurance and comfort. As though reading her thoughts, he reached over and took her hand.

As the preacher presented his sermon, the sounds of rains against the great windows threatened to overpower his voice. Tessa felt an uneasiness; her attention scattered. She thought he would never finish. At last the closing prayer was said and they stood to sing, "A Shelter in the Time of Storm." The selection was most appropriate.

After the benediction, they met the Walshes in the foyer and explained that they would not be joining them for dinner.

"You go right on, kids," Mina said. "We're having chicken and dumplings. Nothing fancy."

"Mama can keep it simmering on the back burner for you," Pauline added.

"I have no idea how long we'll be," Gaven told them.

Russ was helping Mina on with her coat. "You don't owe us an explanation, Gaven," he said kindly. "Our home is yours same as it is Tessa's. Come and go as you please."

"Thank you, Russ. We both appreciate it so much."

The men of the church were running through the rain to bring their automobiles to the entrance to pick up wives and children. The process was taking too much time. Tessa wanted to run through the rain to the parking lot with Gaven, but he made her wait. "There's no sense in your getting soaked," he told her.

She watched from inside the foyer doors at the top of the stone steps as car after car came up and stopped. The rain, blown by a sharp north wind, showed no sign of letting up.

Finally, there was the red roadster. Gaven jumped out and came up the steps for her, holding the large umbrella for her to walk beneath. The strong wind nearly ripped it from his hands. As he opened the door she jumped in, but not before she stepped into icy rushing water over her ankles.

Gaven was forced to drive slowly not only because of the deep standing water, but because the rain was almost blinding.

"I'll take Main all the way to Archer," he said as he strained to see where the curbs were. "That should be the safest route in this mess."

"Oh Gaven, how will they ever survive this?"

He didn't answer. Presently as they sloshed through the muddy roads around the Greenwood area, Tessa leaned forward and peered hard through the rain. They were at Chloe and Willard's tent, but the big square tent was no longer standing.

Chapter 10

"I knew something was wrong," Tessa barely whispered as she gazed at the heap of canvas lying lifeless beneath the pelting rain. "I had a knowing deep inside."

Gaven leaned across her to get a better look. "Roll down the window. It's so hard to make out..."

She did as he asked. The view was clearer through the falling rain than through the steamy glass.

"What do you think happened?" she asked. "The wind?"

"I'm not sure."

"Where do you think they are?"

"I don't know that either, but Preacher Sam and Mama Sue will know."

Tessa released a sigh. "Of course. They're probably there safe and dry."

"And warm."

She cranked the window back up as Gaven drove on. Further down the street they could make out several men in oilcloth slickers scurrying about.

"What in heaven's name are those men doing out in this rain?" Tessa again cranked the window down. "Look Gaven. Another tent is down."

At this announcement, Gaven stopped the car. "Call out to them," he told her.

She cupped her hands to her mouth and shouted, "Hey there! What's going on?"

The men stopped and turned to look. Now she could see one was Willard. He gave a wave, said something to the others, and made his way through the mud to the car. Leaning over to look in the window, he said, "Howdy, Miss Tessa, Gaven. Good to see you."

"Kind of a wet day to be out," Gaven said. "What happened here?"

"They's been carloads of no-count drunk kids driving through here every so often. Yelling, throwing things. You know how drunks is. But last night they got a little carried away."

Tessa was appalled. "White kids did this?"

Willard nodded. "Yes'm they did. We trying to get them tents back up best we can, 'fore everything gets soaked and ruined. Bad enough with just the rain. Now this."

"How many?" Gaven wanted to know.

"Four of 'em."

"Four shelters down that were already inadequate." Anger burned inside Tessa. Why did there have to be such senseless hate? "When did all this happen?"

"Just 'fore daylight. Come through here driving like wild men. They just cut the guy-ropes and then jump back in they cars and high-tail it off."

"Is Chloe with Mama Sue?"

"She is. Y'all go on over there. The coffee's on. We be there directly. One more to go."

"I'll let Tessa off and come back to help," Gaven said.

"Ain't no sense you doing that. Got enough drowned rats out here." Looking over his shoulder at the men working, he chuckled at his own lame joke. "I gotta get back over there now. They needs me."

His wave flicked rainwater from his slicker onto Tessa's face, but she barely noticed. "What are you going to do?" she asked as she cranked the window closed once again.

"Maybe Preacher Sam has a pair of old shoes I can borrow. I'd like to help if I can."

Due to some strange miracle, Preacher Sam's house had sustained only partial damage during the riot. No one had been able to explain why the fire stopped after burning only the front half while other houses burned to the ground. Using what supplies they could find, neighbors had worked to at least get the house enclosed before winter. They had hoped they would be allowed to completely refinish the front without a permit, but permission from city hall had been denied.

The house was full when they arrived. Rotund Mama Sue was playing hostess to them all. She came to the back porch to let in her two most recent guests.

Chloe greeted Tessa with open arms, then looked over at Gaven. "What you doing bringing this little darling out in weather like this?"

"I was worried about you, Chloe." Tessa patted her midsection. "I just had this feeling—right here."

"We all right. Come on in here. Mama Sue, this little gal don't like no coffee, so get her hot cocoa and coffee for her feller."

As they stepped inside the large cheery kitchen, Gaven said, "I'm not staying, Chloe. That is, if someone can get me a pair of old shoes."

"Now what you talking about? You all dressed in your Sunday-go-to-meeting duds. You ain't going back out in that mess."

Mama Sue turned from the stove. "Chloe can't you see that man mean business. He gonna go out there whether or no."

"You're right," Gaven assured her.

"Tessa, honey, you stir this cocoa so it don't get too hot on the bottom. Mr. Gaven, we got a slicker and a pair of galoshes right here on the porch."

As Gaven pulled off his nice fedora and his raincoat, Chloe took them to hang them up, taking Tessa's coat as well. In a matter of minutes, he had donned the slicker and black galoshes—which were two sizes too big—and was back out to join the others.

Presently Mama Sue returned to the kitchen and took the large stirring spoon from Tessa's hand. "We sure appreciate y'all coming over," she said, her voice cheery as though nothing had happened. She took a mug, filled it with hot cocoa and handed it to Tessa. "Here you go. Warm your innards."

"Mama Sue, when will all this ever be over?"

"When will all what be over?"

The woman's perpetual joy was exasperating. "All this mess, all this trouble." Tessa felt like little Vega when she stamped her feet to get her own way. She wanted to stamp her feet and scream and pitch a fit. All this was so unfair. So wrong.

Mama Sue lay down the stirring spoon and turned to put her ample arm around Tessa's shoulder. "Oh sugar, you all upset. Come over here." Turning off the fire, she led Tessa to the kitchen table and pulled out one of the wooden chairs. "Sit down honey." When Tessa was seated, she drew up another chair for herself.

"Let Mama Sue tell you something. When troubles be over, you be in heaven with sweet Jesus. Don't you know that? Don't be no trouble there, but they always be trouble on this side."

"But this is too much. How dare they come in here and destroy what little shelter you have?"

"Now sugar, just think about it." She patted Tessa's hand as though she were a little child. "What be worse? To have no shelter, or have no heart? Chloe and Willard be far better off with a tent falling on they heads than those empty-hearted folk what cut the ropes. Don't you know that?"

Of course, Tessa knew. But she still couldn't bear to see her friends hurt any more than they already had. "Maybe we can get one of the constables to be on duty over here," she said, not wanting to answer Mama Sue's direct question.

"Maybe. Maybe they be a constable here. Maybe they catch a bunch of drunk kids. Maybe they even put 'em in jail." She patted her hefty bosom. "I still be the only one responsible for what goes on inside this heart. Can't be no room for no tiny little root of bitterness." Her clear dark eyes studied Tessa's face making Tessa uncomfortable. "Can't be no room in you either, child. Tiny roots grow mighty big, mighty fast. I tries to keep weeding 'em out while they is tiny and easy to pluck."

From the living room came sounds of the pump organ playing gentle strains of "Amazing Grace." Then the voices joined in like a heavenly choir. Mama Sue began to hum softly. Chloe looked around the door frame that led to the living room. "Come on in here and join us, you two."

"Bring your hot cocoa," Mama Sue said. "Let's go praise Jesus."

———◉———

AFTER THREE DAYS OF cold, wet weather, sunny Indian summer returned once again. Gaven suggested the two of them drive to Mohawk Park the next Saturday. "While the warm weather holds," he said.

They first made a stop at the Coney Islander and bought hot dogs slathered in chili resting in little cardboard boats. These were placed in a paper sack and Gaven put them in the back seat. The aroma filled the car as he drove out Highway 66 to Sheridan Road. The rain-washed skies were a brilliant blue, and the sunshine lent a glow to the golden trees.

As they wheeled around the corner onto Sheridan Road, he slowed and then pulled off to the side. Tessa glanced around. "Why are we stopping?"

He opened his door and stepped out. "Scoot over here, Tessa. I'm going to teach you how to drive."

"But Gaven, I don't need to learn to drive. I'm not even sure I want to." This machine seemed much too big and unfriendly for her liking.

"It's simple. Nothing to it. This isn't like Russ's old Model T. Self-starter, easy to handle. Give it a try."

"I don't think I can even reach the clutch."

"Don't you think I know that my fiancé is a tiny little thing? I just happened to have a pillow here in the back." And he did. Seeing him pulling out the pillow and arranging it in the driver's seat made her laugh. He'd thought of everything. How could she say no?

It took a few adjustments to get the pillow where she needed it. At first she tried sitting on it, but where she really needed it was behind her back. Now she was able to reach the pedals and see out as well. Learning to work the clutch and gearshift was tricky, but he had her stop and start a few times till she had it down smooth.

"Great," Gaven encouraged. "That's great."

As they sailed along down Sheridan Road past the Spartan Airplane Factory, and on past the airport, she felt a wonderful surge of power. "You'll tell me when to turn, won't you?" she asked.

"Keep going down Sheridan and we'll drive around Mohawk Park. There won't be much traffic out here and you can practice."

By the time she'd driven through the winding roads of the large park for the third time, she found she was quite relaxed. "I never thought it could be this easy."

Again, Gaven had her stop the car and start it several times, directing her how to park, how to corner, and how to pass. "You'll be able to get your license in no time," he told her.

"My license?" She could hardly believe it. Tessa Jurgen, the girl from the country, with her own driver's license. Wait till Mama heard about this.

"I've been thinking," Gaven was saying as she drove up to the parking lot of the zoo and stopped the car. "After we're married, there may be days when you can leave me off at school, then drive out to the university yourself for your classes."

"But I could take the trolley," she insisted.

"You could, and some days you may have to, but not always."

"Gaven do you really believe I'll be attending there next term?"

"I haven't a doubt," he said lightly. She wondered how he could be so sure. He hopped out and came around to open her door, grabbing the sack of chili dogs as he did so. "You're a good driver; you learn quick. But then I knew you would."

He led her to a picnic table where they ate the messy chili dogs, laughing and talking in the warm sunshine. Later, they walked along among the cages looking at the many animals there.

"I wish they didn't have to be caged," Tessa said as they viewed a magnificent tawny tiger. His regal head was held high in spite of his imprisonment. "I wish I could see him in his natural state, roaming free."

"That's your tender compassion talking," Gaven said, putting his arm about her and pulling her close. "You seem to be endowed with an ample supply."

She turned to him. "I'm not so sure about that."

"What does that mean?"

"I still feel anger inside at the ones who cut down the tents last week. I'm not sure I'd have compassion for them."

"When push comes to shove, dear little Tessa, you might be surprised at what's deep inside of you."

"You mean how much bitterness is inside me?"

He shook his head. "You're angry and that's understandable. Those are your friends who were affected. But the compassion inside you is much bigger."

"I hope you're right."

"I know I'm right." Then he enfolded her into his arms and kissed her right there in front of that regal tiger.

Chapter 11

The rotations at the store moved Tessa around from accessories, to lingerie, to women's dresses. By the time she returned to dry goods, all the woolens and flannels were out, and the summer sheers had been put in the back stockroom. Although these bolts were considerably heavier than the regular cottons, Tessa didn't really mind. With the change in weather the work was more pleasant, and with each passing day there was less pain in her arm. If anything, the change had helped her to see that every department had its ups and downs.

Floy had also been rotated and lunch relief was switched around as well, so they saw less of one another throughout the day. When they met in the elevator one morning, Floy wanted to know if Tessa had yet been assigned to housewares.

"Not yet," Tessa told her.

"I don't know how you do it. Charmed life, I guess. The absolute dullest place in the entire store and you have yet to experience it."

Tessa knew it wasn't as dull as Floy put on, but her friend loved to exaggerate. They walked together to the cloak room where they hung their coats and hats.

"It'll come sooner or later," Tessa told her.

"You'll be married and out of here before it happens. Just wait and see."

Silently, Tessa hoped she was right.

Floy pulled a package of chewing gum from her bag. She held out a stick to Tessa. Tessa shook her head. They'd been told repeatedly not to chew gum while working, but Floy said she couldn't live without her gum. "Will you be walking to the trolley after work?" she asked as she began chomping on the fresh stick.

"Not tonight. Gaven's picking me up. We're going to look at an apartment one of his fellow teachers told him about."

"Ah, now that sounds romantic." Floy patted her hair as she rolled her eyes. "Looking for your first little love nest together."

"I'll let you know how romantic it is, after I see what the place looks like," Tessa remarked.

Floy stopped and gave Tessa a hard stare, then gave a little laugh. "You're just joking. I can see it in your eyes. You'd follow that guy anywhere."

"Floy, you may be right." She hurried off to report to her post. "See you later."

To Tessa's delight, Mattie Dunbar stopped by the dry goods department that afternoon with both children. Thankfully, store traffic was light when they arrived. Lucie was carrying her favorite doll, Sophia. After hugs from both the children, Lucie announced that Sophia had wanted to come along. "She misses you like I do," Lucie said in her matter-of-fact way.

"I'm glad she came along," Tessa told her. She half expected Wesley to make fun of Lucie's pretending, but he refrained. "Tell me how you've been doing," she said.

"I've been working harder on my studies," Wesley said. "Just ask Mrs. Dunbar if I have." He looked up at his nanny for her affirmation.

"He's telling the truth, Miss Jurgen. Even his arithmetic scores are higher."

"I'm proud of you, Wes. I knew you had it in you. You can have high scores all through school right into college. It's something you can do for yourself—because you have the will."

He nodded. "I know."

"Sadella's getting married." Lucie sidled closer to Tessa not wanting to be left out of the conversation. "I'm going to have a long white dress and I'll carry a basket of flowers down the aisle."

"You'll be lovely, Lucie," Tessa assured her.

"I don't want to be in it, but I have to," Wes said with a scowl.

Tessa was puzzled. "Why don't you want to be in the wedding?"

"I don't like Shelby Harland. Father doesn't think he's too swell either, but I heard him say to Mother that Sadella had better grab him while she can. He doesn't think she'll have another chance..."

Tessa put her fingers to her lips. "Wes, you shouldn't repeat what your family says in private. That's unkind."

"Like being a tattle-tale?" Lucie asked.

"Sort of."

"It's rather like gossip," Mrs. Dunbar offered. To Tessa she said, "They're to be married at the Patton mansion on Valentine's Day. I must say, I've never seen the girl look quite so happy as she is now. She and her mother have made several trips to New York to purchase all the trappings. They'll do it up big. Oh my," she said, glancing at her pendant watch. "We must be getting along. Come children. Pole will be waiting out front."

After they were gone, Tessa found herself wondering about the marriage. While she was thankful that Sadella was happy at last, she couldn't help but wonder about Shelby's intentions.

When she told Gaven about it that evening, he agreed with her. She'd not told him about the incident with Sadella at the accessories counter a few days ago, because she kept thinking it couldn't really be true. From what she learned from Mattie and the children, the wedding plans were definite.

"When he was with us that night in the Walsh's kitchen," Tessa said, "he seemed so despondent. Now he's practically married. What do you think?"

Gaven shook his head. "They're much alike, those two. So spoiled. If I were to guess, I'd say Sadella made a play for him, and in his grief, he took the bait."

"Do you think he loves her?" Tessa wanted to know.

"He's always been such a playboy, who can tell. I didn't think he was actually in love with Clarette, but he seemed to think he was."

The apartment they went to look at was the upstairs of a house on Elwood Street owned by a widow who'd lost two sons in the war. The miniature kitchen reminded Tessa of her garage apartment at the Patton place. The addition of an outside stair created a private entrance. A screened-in porch was situated just off the bedroom. Tessa envisioned the two of them sitting out there talking and sipping lemonade on a steamy summer night. It seemed just right, but Tessa could tell Gaven was hesitant.

The owner, Mrs. Ireton was congenial, and didn't appear to be the meddling type.

"We're not getting married until after Christmas," he told her. "It would be unfair to ask you to hold it for us. We're just looking right now anyway."

"Do you think the rate is unfair?" Her tone was concerned and somewhat motherly. "I've studied what others are asking and I thought I'd set a fair price."

"It's quite fair, Mrs. Ireton, but as I said, we're only looking. We hadn't planned to make any decisions today."

As they returned to the Walsh's house, Tessa ventured to ask him what the problem was. She thought if they rented it now, Gaven could leave the boarding house and move right in. "Was there something about it you didn't like?"

"I like it a lot."

"You want to tell me?"

He was quiet a moment. "Remember that Sunday in church when you felt something was wrong with Chloe?"

"I remember."

"Something inside me now tells me we should wait a while." He glanced over at her. "Are you able to trust that?"

She reached over to touch his arm. "I would trust you with my life."

He pulled the car to a stop in front of the Walsh bungalow, then surprised her taking her face in his hands and gently kissing her. "I don't know what I ever did to deserve you, Tessa. I must be the most blessed man in the whole world."

———————⬥———————

PER GAVEN'S INSTRUCTIONS, Tessa dressed in heavy warm clothes for their next trip to the Glenn Pool, then he covered her with two wool blankets as well. Tessa felt like a little caterpillar in a warm cocoon. Even though all the curtain shades were pulled down and fastened tight, cold air still whipped through the old truck as they bumped along the rutted roads.

At first Gaven tried to talk her into staying with Chloe for the day. "I won't even stay to visit with your family," he told her. "I'll go down, load the supplies and drive right back."

Chloe and Willard added their opinions, because they would have loved to have her spend the day with them. But she wouldn't hear of it. Wherever Gaven went, she wanted to be right by his side.

"And besides," she reminded him, "I'm due for another fitting for my wedding dress. You don't want me to put that off do you?"

She knew she had him; there were no more arguments. But he insisted they fill two thermoses with hot cocoa, and that she be bundled up against the cold. Even though the air was sharp, the sun was bright. Being wrapped up in the old truck made her think of the day she rode to Tulsa in the vegetable truck. It had been almost a year ago. Once Pastor Stedman learned about Tessa's father's plan to give her to Hod Latham in marriage, he immediately set about to get her out of the county. The delivery truck that stopped twice a week at Hargis Mercantile was the escape vehicle for her.

Now riding safe by Gaven's side, she told him the whole story in detail. Even to the point where the delivery boy had tried to steal a kiss.

That's when she found herself, bags in hand, walking through the sleet storm on her way to the Patton mansion.

"And that's when I first saw you along Riverside Drive," Gaven said. "I thought you were just a little girl who'd run away from home. If I'd known then what I know now, I would have *made* you get in the car."

Tessa laughed. "If I'd known then what I know now, I would have jumped in without your asking."

When they arrived at the Stedman's home, Siegrid and Vega came running out coatless, falling all over one another trying to talk at once. They were excited to see Tessa, they were excited about the upcoming wedding, but they also had another surprise, they said.

"What is it?" Tessa asked. "Did the barn-cat have kittens?"

Vega bounced up and down like a jack-in-the-box. "Better than that. Better than that! May I tell, Siegrid?"

Siegrid solemnly shook her head. "We promised. A promise is a promise."

"Aren't you going to say hello to Gaven?" Tessa said.

Vega then went running to him and he lifted her into the air, which made her squeal.

The back door was open now and Pastor was there, smoothing his mustache and smiling broadly. "Gracious me, what's all this squealing out here? Sounds like a stuck hog."

That, of course, only made Vega giggle harder. Tessa watched Gaven with her sisters and was amazed that he seemed to sense he had to approach Siegrid more slowly than Vega.

The kitchen was filled with wonderful aromas of spiced cider and popcorn. The girls had spent the morning learning how to make popcorn balls, and the result was a wooden bowl piled high with the snowy-white balls in the center of the kitchen table.

While Mama and Edith were trying to greet them, Vega was trying to explain how they'd made the sticky balls. It was a happy madhouse, and Tessa loved every minute of it.

When they were finally all sitting in the parlor drinking mugs of hot, spiced cider and munching on the sweet popcorn balls, Pastor explained that Mama had something to tell them.

"Mama? This secret is *your* secret? The girls didn't say that." Tessa gazed at her mother who seemed to have grown younger and more beautiful before her very eyes. The worry lines were gone from her sky-blue eyes; the strain erased from her face. "What is it, Mama?" Tessa whispered.

"Is not to be secret. Dat's vat Edith says. I vant to tell everybody." She pressed her hands to her heart. "Jesus now is right here."

Tessa felt a sudden rush of joy. She jumped up from where she was sitting and knelt by her mother's side. "I've been praying this would happen. I'm so happy for you, Mama."

"I thought I was Christian." She shrugged. "Now I understand, Jesus died for me."

"You can't stay in this house for very long and not know about the gift of salvation," Tessa said.

"*Ya*. Is true. But you, my tiny little one, led the way for all of this." She spread her hands to take in the Stedman's, the house, but also the love that lived there. "Fine daughter you are, Tessa. Fine daughter."

"Oh Mama." Suddenly they were in each other arms, and tears were flowing. Then Siegrid and Vega crawled into the middle; Tessa and Mama opened their arms to let them in.

"Well, MacIntyre," Pastor's booming voice broke into the weeping, "did you ever in your life see such mush? Why you'd think they all cared about one another or something."

"Now Royce," Edith chided.

But no one minded Pastor's kidding, and soon tears and laughter were intermingled. Gaven also gave Mama a hug and expressed his joy at her decision.

Later, while Edith put dinner on the table, Mama and Tessa slipped into the unheated upstairs where Tessa saw how the wedding dress was coming along. The lace and satin dress was nearing completion, and it looked very similar to the original picture from *Ladies Home Companion*. Mama had begun the task of sewing tiny seed pearls onto the lace.

"When you come Thanksgiving, the hem ve vill mark," Mama said.

"That'll be perfect. I'd like to have it completely done before Christmas. That way if the weather turns bad and we can't get here, I'll rest easy knowing it's all finished."

Over dinner, Pastor wanted to know all the developments in the rebuilding process. Tessa and Gaven explained about the carloads of young people driving through Greenwood causing disruptions and tearing down the tents.

Pastor just shook his head in disbelief. "Ignorance gone to seed," he said. "Empty-headed youngsters with too much time and too much money. I pray they realize their need for the Lord before it's too late."

"Chloe says they have empty hearts."

"Now that's right smart," Pastor agreed. "Hope I get to meet this Chloe."

Gaven glanced at Tessa. "We're hoping that a few of our friends from Greenwood can come to the wedding," he said. "We want to do it without causing a problem within the church. Our pastor is agreeable, but of course there'll be a few members who won't look on it favorably."

Edith smiled at them. "I admire your courage. What a light you are to others in the community."

Before they left that afternoon, Pastor Stedman said, "You kids are bucking some pretty heavy stuff with all you're doing. I feel we need to say a special prayer for you. Edith?"

They were standing in the kitchen. Edith had rinsed out the thermoses and re-filled them with hot apple cider. She handed them to Gaven. "I agree."

So along with Mama and the girls, they formed a circle there in the kitchen while Pastor prayed a prayer of protection round about them. Tessa had never felt more enveloped in love.

The next trip would be on Thanksgiving Day. "And when we come then, we'll be in my car," Gaven told them, "rather than this old jalopy." He waved in the direction of the truck. "It holds plenty of lumber, but it rides like an old buckboard."

"If the weather holds, I may be driving," Tessa said, which made the girls wide-eyed.

"A little thing like you at the wheel?" Pastor said with a deep chuckle. "You can't even reach the clutch."

They were down the steps now and walking to the truck. "With a pillow I can," she countered.

Hearing that comment, Pastor let loose with a loud belly laugh. "I can't wait to see that sight!" he said, slapping his leg.

"You'll see it," Gaven promised. "If not on Thanksgiving, then soon. She's already taken her test for her license—and she passed!"

"Imagine that," Pastor quipped.

"I'm so proud of you, Tessa," Mama said reaching though the truck window to take her hand.

Again, Gaven covered her with the blankets to be sure she would stay warm. He gave the crank a few hard turns and the truck jumped to life. They shouted good-byes over the rumble and roar of the motor.

Gaven had left the order for supplies at the lumber yard on their way in, so the order was pulled and ready to load. The loading took barely thirty minutes. Gaven paid the bill with the money he'd been given.

Gaven was singing before they even reached Lone Grove Crossroads. These drives were giving them plenty of practice, and Tessa learned how to harmonize with him. They were on the first chorus of "Rescue the Perishing," when Gaven stopped in mid-phrase.

"Look there, Tessa. It's a man on the road. Must be in trouble. I'd better stop."

Tessa had been turned in the seat looking at Gaven as they sang together. Now she turned to look at the road. Through the dim dusk the form grew larger, and suddenly the face was clear. That face. That face which haunted Tessa in her nightmares. That horrid, wicked face. Icy fear clutched at her as she screamed, "Don't stop, Gaven! Don't stop! It's Hod Latham!"

Chapter 12

The barrel-chested, bow-legged figure moved to the center of the road waving a battered, greasy, felt hat to flag them down. In a flash, Gaven stepped hard on the accelerator as he swerved to miss the man. The truck hit the deep ruts and lurched. Tessa's heart froze as she slammed against the door.

"Hang on," Gaven said. But the stiff old truck didn't respond so easily, and with a sickening thump, it slammed into Hod Latham throwing him into the side ditch.

At the same moment an explosion sounded. With an instinct born in wartime, Gaven reached out to push Tessa down. "Get down," he ordered. "Someone's shooting at us!"

Tessa scrunched down in the seat as yet another report crackled behind them. Gaven pushed the pedal to the floor demanding the weighted old truck to move faster.

"Must be shooting in the air," he said, "or they'd surely have hit one of the tires."

Tessa shivered at the thought.

After one more shot there was no sound other than the grind of the truck pushing and straining.

"Maybe they won't follow," Gaven said in barely a whisper. His face was white. Even his lips had gone pale. Though a hint of relief sounded in his voice, he didn't let up on the gas.

Slowly, Tessa righted herself to a sitting position. For a good ten minutes, neither of them spoke. Shame swept over Tessa as she realized the danger Gaven was in because of her. She didn't know what to say. If only there were something she could do to make it right again.

Only after he had put several miles between them and the gunshots did Gaven slow the truck somewhat. "Do you think he knew it was you in here?" Tessa knew Gaven was having trouble comprehending all of this.

"He knew." She couldn't bear to say the rest. Not only did he know her whereabouts, but he would pursue her till he had her. That's the kind of man Hod was—slow and dull, but ruthless. For a time she thought she could forget. She dared to believe her past would no longer plague her. But it simply wasn't true. It would always be there. Even the Bible said the sins of the fathers would visit the next generations.

After another long silence, Gaven asked, "Are you all right? You hit that door pretty hard." Only then did the pain in her arm begin to register in her brain. She'd hit her arm which was still healing from the bullet wound of last June. She pulled her hand out from beneath the blanket to reach up and rub her arm. But her hand was shaking, trembling violently with a mind of its own. She struggled to stop the trembling, but it exploded and she was shaking as though gripped with a violent chill.

"Tessa." Gaven said. "Tessa talk to me. Are you all right?"

She tried to speak but she had to clench her teeth to keep them from chattering. All she could do was shake her head.

"Shall I stop?"

No she didn't want him to stop. She shook her head again. She saw the confusion cloud his face. He didn't know whether to rush her home, or to stop and tend to her. Suddenly, he steered the truck off to the side of the road and reached over to pull her into his arms. "Tessa, my darling Tessa. It's all right. Pastor prayed for us, remember? I'm here. I've got you. You're safe with me. I'll take care of you."

Then he opened one of the thermoses and helped her drink the hot cider. She unclenched her teeth to sip, as the spicy hot liquid flowed warm down inside her. At last her jaws relaxed and the trembling ceased. She buried her head in his chest and as he cradled her in his arms, deep heaving sobs replaced the trembling.

"Darling, Tessa. I love you." He took her face in his hands. In the reflection from the headlights and through her tears she could barely see his kind brown eyes. "Do you hear me, Tessa? I love you no matter what!"

From his pocket he pulled out his handkerchief and patted her tears away. "If you're blaming yourself for this mess, I want you to stop it. Do you understand? You're not to blame."

She took the handkerchief and blew her nose. "I've put you in this danger," she said.

"No, Tessa. I've chosen this path to take, no matter what the cost." Softly he kissed one eyelid, and then the other. "No matter what the cost," he repeated softly. "Now you finish that cider and let's get on home."

Even if they had planned to keep quiet about the incident, it never would have worked. Chloe took one look at Tessa and demanded to know what happened. After the lumber was unloaded, they all went to Mama Sue's so they could tell the story.

"I knowed that no-count man wouldn't stay hid forever," Chloe said.

Mama Sue was passing around ample slices of her sweet potato pie, but neither Gaven nor Tessa could eat.

"I 'spects we won't need no more trips to fetch lumber for a time," Willard said. The others in the group agreed. "Cold weather comin' on. Not many permits moving."

"Let's make those decisions as they come," Gaven said. "We're fine. God watched over us. As a matter of fact, we'll be driving down again for Thanksgiving. We can't stop everything just because one lunatic is running loose."

"You right," Preacher Sam put in. "But God don't want us being foolhardy. We supposed to pray for wisdom."

"Mm hm," Mama Sue agreed. "We pray for that right now."

Tonight not even the prayers of her black friends could ease the cold knot inside her. She kept seeing bullets ripping through her beloved Gaven.

At the Walsh house, Tessa prayed everyone would be in bed so she could slip quietly to her room. But Mina, clad in a warm bathrobe, was sitting in the kitchen waiting for them.

Gaven brought Tessa to the back door when they saw the kitchen light.

"Mina," Tessa said, "you didn't have to wait up."

"You've not been this late before," she explained. Her tone and even her expression were apologetic. "I guess you never get loose of worrying about your kids." Then, just as Chloe had, she took a hard look at Tessa and knew something wasn't right. "Did you have a wreck?" she asked coming out of her chair and putting her arms around Tessa.

On a past occasion, Tessa had shared bits and pieces of the story of Hod. So when Gaven merely mentioned the name, she understood. Putting up her hand, she said. "You don't have to tell me all the details. You're both tired. Tessa, I'll fill the hot water bottle and you take a powder to help you sleep."

"I know she's in good hands," Gaven said. "I'll be going."

"What about you, Gaven? Are you all right?" Mina asked him.

"It was a scare, but I'll be fine. I've been shot at many times and lived to tell about it." Gaven moved toward the door. "Tessa, don't forget what I told you."

"I won't forget."

After a hot bath, Tessa crawled into bed which Mina had already warmed with the electric bed-warmer.

"Put the hot water bottle against your midsection," Mina instructed. "It'll help you relax."

But Tessa knew no sleeping powder, no amount of warmth or comfort would help. That face, with the sinister eyes shelved over with craggy black brows, would torment her whether asleep or awake. She knew what Hod was thinking: the only way he could get to her was to get rid of Gaven first.

—————◉—————

"HAVE YOU HEARD ANYTHING I've said in the last five minutes?" Floy asked. Floy was working in accessories so they were able to take their lunch hour together. Floy insisted they go to Kress's and Tessa agreed since she hadn't bothered to pack a lunch. She'd not eaten much of anything since Saturday night.

"I heard you," Tessa insisted. "You were saying how a customer wanted a pair of six-and-a-half gloves when she needed at least a size seven-and-a-half."

"That's what I said a few minutes ago. But then I was telling you about the silk hosiery she tried to return. Honestly, Tessa, they were a sight. Why doesn't she just admit she needs a larger size? Tessa?" She rapped the lunch counter making Tessa jump. "There. See what I mean? You're a million miles away. Something's wrong. What is it?"

"Nothing. If you'll stop scaring me by smacking the counter, I'll be fine."

Floy took a large bite out of her ham sandwich. "You're not yourself, that's for sure," she said around the mouthful. "Look there." She pointed at Tessa's full plate. "You're not eating your sandwich. You're all quiet and sullen. And yesterday I heard that Ila found three mistakes in your sales slips. You may not want to tell me what's wrong, but don't try to deny it's something."

The tears started to burn in Tessa's eyes. She fought them back. "I'm sorry, Floy. You've been such a good friend. You're right, something is wrong, but I can't tell you. Not now anyway."

"Does it have to do with your helping over in Greenwood? I've always thought you and Gaven were taking an awful chance..."

"No. Nothing like that. I don't think anyone even cares anymore that we're helping them."

"I've never seen you this upset. Is there anything I can do to help?"

"Thank you, Floy. There's nothing anyone can do."

"Well, let's at least have Marvin wrap up that sandwich. You may get hungry later today."

Tessa could only nod. Because she knew it would be no different later on. Food had lost its flavor.

As they walked back down Main, Floy said, "Don't tally your till this afternoon until I have a chance to come down and double check it. Okay? Promise me?"

"All right. I promise."

"We don't want you losing your job over this... This whatever it is."

Lose her job? What did a job matter when a life was at stake?

When she and Gaven were driving home together after mid-week Bible study Wednesday night, he too expressed his concern for her.

"You've got to snap out of this, Tessa," he warned. "I don't want you to be sick. Look, we're fine. It was just his lame attempt to frighten us. He can't win. That is, unless you let it get to you."

But she knew it was so much more than a lame attempt. It was just *one* attempt. There was no way she could help Gaven to see. In fact, part of her didn't want him to see.

w

She was just finishing up a sale of red satin the Thursday afternoon following Hod's attack. The customer was planning to sew a Christmas party dress. She wanted red sequins to use for trim.

Suddenly Ila Taylor approached Tessa's counter. "Miss Jurgen. Telephone for you."

Tessa's blood went cold. Absolutely no calls were allowed for employees, except in emergencies.

Tessa turned to the customer. "Excuse me please."

"I'll ring it up for you," Ila said. "You can take your call in the employee lounge."

Woodenly, Tessa took the elevator up to third floor. There was the pedestal phone on the table. She forced her hand to pick up the receiver. "Hello?"

"Tessa." Gaven's voice was strained. "It's the Creek County Sheriff. He's here—at the school—to take me. Tessa, I'm under arrest for hit and run."

Chapter 13

"Tessa. Are you there?"

Tessa sat down in the chair nearest the phone table. She felt as though her gut had been ripped out. "I'm right here, Gaven." So this was how Hod would get him. To have him locked up. Everything inside her wanted to scream out "No! No! Stop this insanity!" She fought down the scream and willed her hands to stop shaking.

"I only have a few minutes, so listen closely," Gaven was saying. "I want you to take the trolley to the school after work and then drive my car back to the Walsh's house. Understand?"

"Yes."

"They won't mind having it at their house for a while. It won't be for very long."

"They won't mind," she repeated.

"This won't take long to straighten out, Tessa. After all, they were shooting at us. It was self-defense."

What they both knew, and could not speak, it would be their word against that of Hod and whomever he had hiding by the side of the road.

"I have my license now," she said. "I'll drive down to the county jail."

"Not alone. Please, Tessa, don't try to go anywhere alone just now. Take Pauline or someone. Promise me?"

"I'm not sure I can promise that, Gaven." She felt herself sitting up a little straighter. "I'll do what's necessary for the situation."

"You're so stubborn. But I love you for it. The key will be in it. One more thing. Talk to Miles Calbert and tell him the situation. He can't represent me, but he may be the only attorney around who can give me the name of someone free of Klan control."

There was that word again. The very thought of the powerful Klan sent icy fingers of fear shooting through her. "I'll talk to him right away," she assured him. "He'll be glad to help us."

"I'm counting on it," he said. Tessa could hear voices talking in the background. Suddenly Gaven's voice was strained again. "I've got to go now Tessa. I love you, my darling. I love you with all my heart."

She was barely able to tell him she loved him too before the hollow click sounded in her ear. For a few minutes she sat there stunned. Then she realized she couldn't finish out the day at the dry goods counter. Keeping her mind on fabrics would be impossible.

How would she know what to do? she wondered. This was no time to fall apart. She would do one thing at a time and trust God to give her the wisdom. First she'd get her coat and hat and handbag. That one thought enabled her to stand and move stiffly to the cloakroom. After pinning on her hat and pulling on her coat she took the elevator back down to first floor.

As she returned to dry goods, Ila gave her a surprised stare. "There are three more hours until quitting time, Miss Jurgen."

"Something's come up. An emergency with my fiancé. I must go."

"I see," she said rather coolly. "You'll be here in the morning?"

"I... I'm not sure." And she really wasn't. She wasn't sure what needed to be done.

"I'll have to speak to Mr. Osborn about this. It's highly irregular. Wait just a moment while I go get him."

Suddenly Tessa realized she could lose her job over this. But what did it matter? "I can't wait. I must leave now." And with that she turned and walked out.

As she rode the trolley to Riverview School, her mind swam with ugly visions of hooded figures coming in the night to take Gaven from the cell and... No, she couldn't. She had to get control. She had to be strong for both of them.

She walked from the trolley stop to the school parking lot where his roadster sat. Seeing the car, seeing the school and knowing he was not there nearly took her breath away. How would she ever get through this?

Before driving off, she felt it would be best to talk to the lady who worked in the school office to tell her she was taking the car.

"Thank you for coming in," Miss Patrick said, her voice heavy with sympathy. "He told me you'd be coming for the car. I want you to know none of us here believe Mr. MacIntyre would ever do anything against the law."

"I appreciate that," Tessa said. "I know Gaven does, too."

"It was so terrible for him... I mean, that it had to happen here in front of the children."

Tessa couldn't answer. Knowing how much Gaven loved his students she knew what Miss Patrick meant. It must have been a nightmare experience.

"Our principal told him we'd have a substitute here for as long as it took for him to get this taken care of."

"Please thank him for me. For both of us."

"We're praying for you."

"Yes. Please do that."

In the back seat of the roadster was her pillow. She had to smile as she thought of him putting in there for her when he decided to teach her to drive. What a gem he was.

She drove straight to the tent where Miles and Lanny worked, but no one was there. The cold had no doubt driven them elsewhere to warmer quarters. But where? Chloe would know. Luckily it was Thursday, Chloe's day off.

Chloe, hearing the car, stuck her head out the opening of her tent home. "Land sakes, child. What you doing over here this time of day? And where's that man of yours?"

"I'm looking for Miles, Chloe." Tessa stepped up into the tent which was cozy warm from the kerosene heater standing in the center.

"They done set up business in the basement of the church. The men cleared out a place and fixed it up right nice. Now you gonna tell me what's going on?" She stopped and took a long look at Tessa. "Something about that Hod fellow, ain't it?"

Tessa nodded. "The Creek County sheriff came and took Gaven, Chloe. He's under arrest as a hit and run driver."

"I mighta knowed." She grabbed her hat and coat from a rack in the corner. "I was just about ready to go down to Mama Sue's. Some of us be stitching a quilt together. Let's stop there first so they can be praying, when we go find Miles."

Her decisiveness was like a balm giving Tessa an inner boost. They hopped in the car and drove the few blocks to Mama Sue's house where a few women were sitting around the quilting frame. When they heard the news, they wanted to stop and pray just then, but Tessa insisted she go on to talk with Miles.

"Let me go with you," Preacher Sam said. "I wants to hear what he has to say about the situation."

"No way you going without me," Chloe added quickly. To the others, she said, "I'll be back shortly. Keep the coffee hot, and don't stop praying."

Miles' office was in a cramped corner of the church basement. Thick law books were piled and scattered about everywhere. Tessa watched the attorney's face twist into a worried scowl as she explained the details of the encounter with Hod at the crossroads. "Did you hear any shots hit the truck?" he asked.

She shook her head. "Gaven thought they must have shot in the air only to scare us."

"He was probably right." Miles scribbled in a notebook as he spoke. "You say this man's a bootlegger?"

"He's had stills as long as I've known anything about him," Tessa told him.

"Some two-bit operation back in the hills?" Miles asked.

"It was. Now Pastor Stedman has heard that Hod's connected with some people over in Arkansas."

Miles scribbled down that information too, pursing his lips as he did so. "Interesting. Sounds like he's a little man who's getting deeper into big trouble. Wish I had a connection with the Feds."

Chloe reached over to touch Tessa's arm. "You gonna call your big Swede cousin to tell him about Gaven's arrest?"

Tessa hadn't even thought of Erik yet. She hadn't been able to think of much of anything. "I should. I can do that tonight."

"When you do," Chloe added, "ask him if that wife of his know any agents. She be from New York."

"Who's this?" Miles pulled off his glasses. "You have a relative from New York? That could be an answer."

"She's talking about my cousin, Erik Torsten," Tessa explained. "He married the reporter from New York who came last summer to cover the story of the riot."

"The lady kidnapped by the Klan?"

"That's her."

"I didn't realize she married your cousin. Are you in contact with them?"

"Erik's taken over the newspaper in Bartlesville. Actually, I've not talked with them in several months."

Preacher Sam, who'd been quietly listening up till now, spoke up, "Mr. Erik would want to know his buddy's been throwed in jail. Don't you think, Miss Tessa?"

They were right of course. Erik and Gaven had been war buddies and were very close. She'd have to call him right away. And perhaps Clarette could help as well. "I'll call as soon as I get home."

"You let me know when you find out anything," Miles said. "Meanwhile I'll make a few telephone calls to see what I can learn from my end. Maybe we can get Gaven out on bail."

Miles made it sound so simple to place those calls. But Tessa knew since telephone service still hadn't been restored to the area, the lack of phones presented hardships for all of Greenwood.

As they stood to go, Tessa asked, "Did anything ever come of the idea for volunteers to assist with the building permits?"

Mile shook his head. "I have a feeling the vocal Mrs. Patton put a stop to it before it could ever start."

"I thought so."

"Also," Miles added, "something tells me Mr. Patton and some of his cohorts are wielding their power over city hall to keep the process slowed."

IF GAVEN HAD BEEN THERE he would have been proud of how neatly she parked the roadster in front of the Walsh house. In fact, she'd done quite well coming through town stopping at all the stoplights. As soon as the motor was off, Mina came running out the front door drying her hands on a dishtowel, her face stricken. It was barely four in the afternoon.

"Tessa what is it?" Mina came down the steps of the wide porch toward Tessa, wrapping her in her arms. "Come on inside and sit down, my dear. Then you can tell me everything."

"I can't sit down yet, Mina. May I make a long-distance call? I may have to make two."

"Why of course, Tessa." She pulled open the screen door and let Tessa go in first.

When they were inside the cozy front room Tessa turned to Mina. "But I may not be able to pay you for them. I may not have a job any longer."

"If you never paid us a cent for anything ever, you're welcome to all we have. I thought you knew that."

As Tessa pulled off her coat and hat and started toward the coat closet. Mina said, "Tessa. Where's Gaven?"

It hurt so bad to say it, but she would have to repeat it many more times. "He's under arrest."

Mina's hand flew to her mouth to stifle the gasp.

"The Creek Country sheriff came for him at the school."

"Not in front of the children."

"In front of everyone."

"Oh my dear Tessa." As Mina wrapped her in a comforting hug, the tears Tessa had fought to restrain came flowing forth unchecked. "We'll do anything we can to help. You know that." Mina drew her to the sofa and made her sit down, then pulled a clean hankie from her apron pocket. "There, there. Everything will be all right. You'll see."

But Tessa wasn't so sure. Without any warning, that jail could be surrounded by Klansmen and the authorities would be helpless to stop it. But there was no time for her to be blubbering. She straightened herself and wiped her eyes on the hankie. "I'm so grateful for you, Mina. Thank you for being here for me."

"You make your calls now, and I'll fix you a cup of tea."

"I'd like that."

She dreaded to have to alarm Erik. But it was only right that he be informed. Once again she had to tell the story, detail by detail, only this time through all the crackling and static on the lines. The connection was horrible and she could barely hear him, but there was no mistaking his anger.

"That low-down ornery Latham has got to be stopped," he fairly shouted through the line at her. "We put this paper to bed tomorrow, Tessa, then Clarette and I will drive down there on Saturday. We'll do whatever needs to be done. I know my dad can help raise the bail. We gotta get Mac out of that place."

"Don't come tomorrow, Erik. I won't be here."

"You won't what?"

"I won't be in Tulsa. I have Gaven's car and I have my license now so I'm driving to Sapulpa tomorrow."

"Not by yourself, I hope."

"I don't know yet." And she didn't. In fact, she only that very moment decided to go tomorrow to be with him. She had to go.

"You better not. It's too dangerous."

"Erik, don't worry about me, let's think about Gaven. Is Clarette there?"

"Clarette's here in the office. We do this crazy newspaper thing together."

"Ask her if she knows any federal agents back east."

"Ask her if she knows who?"

Tessa paused to let the awful crackling pass. "Federal agents. Does she know any federal agents?"

"I don't know. I'll ask her."

Tessa could hear him talking to Clarette and from the background she could hear Clarette answering. Presently, Clarette was on the line. "Tessa. Hi there. The answer to your question is yes, I do know an agent. A real doozy. Top of the line. Never been bought off."

Chapter 14

The request seemed like such a long shot, Tessa wasn't sure why she was bothering to ask Clarette about it. It wasn't clear what good Miles thought it would do to have a federal agent come into the situation.

Hesitantly she asked Clarette, "Can you get hold of that agent? Would he be able to help us clear out here in Oklahoma?"

"It may take a day or so, but I can find him. I don't know what help you're needing."

"I'm not sure either, but if he agrees talk to us would you leave word here with the Walshes, or with Pastor Stedman? I want to put him in touch with an attorney named Miles Calbert."

"Just give me the telephone number of this Calbert fellow."

"I can't, Clarette. There are no telephones in Greenwood."

"Okay. I understand. We'll get word to you somehow just as soon as we know something."

As Tessa and Clarette rang off, Mina brought the steaming tea. Now the next step was to get hold of Pastor and Edith and inform them. She took a big breath and then drank a sip of the tea.

"One step at a time," Mina said softly. "Take it one step at a time, and you'll be able to do whatever needs to be done."

She nodded and picked up the pedestal phone one more time.

Tessa wasn't sure which upset Pastor more, the fact that Gaven was in jail, or the fact that she was planning to drive down there. He tried his best to talk her out of it, but it was useless. Her mind was made up.

"I'm starting out in the morning no matter what," she said. "No one will know me in Gaven's roadster."

"Well, then," he said, "drive out here to our place first. Then you and I can drive to Sapulpa together. Will you at least agree to that?"

She thought about his idea. Having him with her at the jail would be a blessing. "All right. I'll be there early."

"Edith and your mama will have breakfast ready."

w

At supper that evening it was the same ordeal all over again. Telling the story and watching the awful expressions of anguish as Russell and Pauline heard the news. Russ, like Pastor Stedman, was insistent she not go alone. "If I didn't have to be on the job tomorrow, I'd be right beside you in that car."

"I'll be fine, really."

"I could take off work," Pauline put in. "I could go."

"I may not come back until Sunday."

"That's all right," Pauline said. "Someone can cover for me."

Tessa couldn't see what difference it would make, and she certainly didn't want to put anyone else's life in danger. But in the end they won out. Or at least so it seemed.

Early the next morning Pauline awakened with swollen, flaming red, tonsils. She would be going nowhere. And Mina would have to tend to her. So, before dawn, Tessa packed her things and prepared to leave.

"If anything happens to you," Russ said as he put her small valise in the back of the car, "I'll never forgive myself."

"Just pray for me." She adjusted her pillow and crawled in and closed the door.

"Kiddo," Russ said with his cocked grin. "Since you came into our lives, I've increased my prayer life four-fold!" He patted her shoulder. Just then, Mina came scurrying out with a thermos of cocoa for her.

"I probably won't have time to stop and drink that," Tessa protested as she accepted the kind gesture.

"But then you never know," Mina said.

Tessa knew the "mother" in Mina wanted to do something, in the same way that she had go to the jail today. She knew it would solve nothing, but she had to go. She had to be there with Gaven, if even for only a few moments.

A rosy sunrise lit the eastern sky as she crossed the bridge over the muddy slow-moving Arkansas River and drove south of the city. Soon the sun slipped up over the horizon touching the golden cottonwoods and scarlet scrub oaks with light.

Though she enjoyed this new sensation of independence, by the end of the first hour, her legs were quite tired. It was a strain to stretch to reach the foot pedal. Driving wasn't all that difficult; fighting the deep ruts was the hard part. This was the first time she'd not been on paved streets, other than the dirt roads in Greenwood. But even there, the ruts were nothing like this. She was just thankful it wasn't muddy or icy.

As the roadster neared Lone Grove Crossroads a shiver coursed through her. In her mind she heard the echoes of gun shots, knowing full well Hod could have killed Gaven that night and then he could have dragged her away. *Why didn't he?* she wondered. But then why should he be in a hurry, as long as he knew where she was? And why should he commit murder when he could let the law take care of Gaven?

Vega and Siegrid were quite distraught at the thought of Gaven being locked up in jail. They knew full well who Hod Latham was and what he represented. But they couldn't understand why Hod wasn't locked up rather than Gaven. Tessa didn't have the time to explain. She didn't even want to stop and eat, but Edith and Mama insisted. It was like having two mothers looking out for her. And three counting Mina. Mama had prepared a shoe box of homemade ginger cookies for her to take to Gaven.

At last she and Pastor were in the roadster heading out toward Sapulpa. She offered to let him drive, but he just laughed.

"What? And miss seeing a little peanut maneuver a big old automobile? Not on your life."

The drive straight down Route 66 from Tulsa to Sapulpa would have been a much shorter distance. But now she was glad Pastor had talked her into coming to get him first. Once she got a glimpse of granite-colored stone jailhouse at the end of Sapulpa's short main street, she realized she couldn't have gone in there alone.

The old jail must have been built during Indian Territory days. Tessa could hardly believe the decrepit condition. As she pulled to a stop in front of the building, she wondered how she would get through this.

Pastor Stedman came around to open her door and help her out. Together they walked across the sidewalk to the small building. Pastor pushed the wooden door open and allowed her to go in. Tessa was surprised that the inside wasn't much warmer than outdoors. A small kerosene heater stood in the corner. The door on the opposite wall no doubt led to the cells. Gaven was right there. Just past that door. Her heart was racing.

To their left was a battered wooden desk. A trim middle-aged man was tilted back in a wooden swivel chair with his boot-clad feet propped on the desk. Yellowed, tattered wanted posters lined the wall behind his head. He didn't appear surprised to see them.

"Come to see the school teacher I take it?" he said. The worn boots hit the floor with a harsh thud.

"Yes we have," Pastor said, stepping right up to the desk. Now Tessa was more thankful than ever that he was with her.

"I'm Sheriff Bynum. I'm the one who brought in this hit-and-run driver. Serious offence using an automobile as a weapon."

Tessa bit her tongue. Miles had warned her not to say a thing that might incriminate Gaven further.

"What's in the box? A derringer?" The sheriff gave a horsey laugh.

Tessa saw nothing funny. "Just cookies." She moved forward to stand right by pastor's side. "May we see Mr. MacIntyre?"

"Well now, I don't know. Let's see what's in that box." He reached out his hand and Tessa offered up the shoebox to him. As she watched him open it, she was suddenly swept back to the moment when she stood alone in the Tulsa county jail. The guard there took the cake Chloe had baked for Jasper and hacked it to pieces with his pocket knife as he "searched" for contraband. The few moments she spent with Jasper and his friend, Strapper, that afternoon was the last time she ever saw Jasper alive.

"Mmm. Ginger cookies. My most favorite kind of cookie. You won't mind if I have a few." It was a statement, not a question. He unfolded the tissue paper that Edith had so lovingly and carefully arranged around the cookies. Fishing around, he pulled out several of the largest cookies and placed them on his desk. He dug to the bottom of the box, breaking cookies in the process, as though there were surely something dangerous hidden beneath all those cookies. Finally, he took hold of the tissue paper and lifted it out of the box entirely, looking down into the empty box. Satisfied, he pushed the tissue-cradle of cookies back in crushing more cookies as he did so.

Tessa felt her anger rising at his senseless act of arrogance. "May we see Mr. MacIntyre?" she asked again.

"Now now, don't get in a all-fired hurry." Slowly he replaced the lid on the shoebox and handed it back to Tessa. "All safe, ma'am," he said with a smirk. Reaching down, he pulled open a lower drawer of the desk and pulled out a jingling ring of keys. They clanked as he rose, walked to the door, and unlocked it.

"You have fifteen minutes," he said.

Tessa felt Pastor stiffen. "Surely we can have more than fifteen minutes. We're not bothering anyone."

"Fifteen minutes," came the harsh reply. "Take it or leave it."

There were only two cells—one on one side, one on the other—with a small run in between. It was clammy cold. The cell was small and dirty. Thankfully, no other prisoners were locked up just now. There was Gaven standing against the bars, his face wreathed in a smile of relief at the sight of her. "Tessa. I heard your voice."

She wanted to rush to him, but the sheriff was in the way. He opened the small metal door-within-the-door, to pass the box to him. "Here's you a little goody from your purty girl."

Gaven took the box without taking his eyes off Tessa and set it on the floor. He was dressed in one of his tweed jackets, his gabardine slacks and nice shirt, but all were rumpled since he'd slept in them. His fedora lay on the small metal cot.

"Fifteen minutes," the sheriff repeated as he turned to go.

Once he was out of the way, she stepped over to Gaven and reached through to take his hands. Gently taking her hands he pressed them to his face closing his eyes as he did so. The stubble of a day's-growth of beard felt rough on her palms. "Tessa thank you for coming to me." Feeling his tears on her fingertips, she couldn't hold back her own tears.

"I couldn't have stayed away."

"But your work... What about your job?"

"I just left. How could I work when you're here?"

He nodded. "I understand."

Pastor reached through the bars and patted Gaven's shoulder gently. "God's watching over you, Gaven." His voice choked. "Plenty of people are praying."

"All of Greenwood is praying," Tessa added. "I've called Erik. Miles said..."

Pastor touched her arm and put his finger to his lips, nodding toward the outer office. In a louder voice, he said, "In fact I think we ought to be praying right now. This is a terrible mess. Just a terrible mess." Mouthing the words, he told them, "You two whisper."

Stepping closer to the door, which was slightly ajar, Pastor prayed in a loud voice, calling down all the forces of heaven into that old jail. Meanwhile, Tessa quickly and quietly told Gaven what Miles said about getting a federal agent—one who couldn't be bought off—to be pulled in on the case.

Gaven too was a little confused, but said, "I trust Miles. He knows the law, and he's as honest as the day is long."

She filled him in on what Clarette had said about an agent, and that Tessa would be hearing from them shortly. "I'm staying over until Sunday, then I'll drive back to Tulsa early Sunday morning. Erik and Clarette are driving down Sunday afternoon. I'll know more then."

"Good old Erik," he said, still tightly clasping her hands. "I'm so glad you thought to call him."

"Erik said his father may be able to raise the bail money."

Gaven shook his head. "There's no bail, Tessa."

"What? How could there be no bail?"

"I have no idea, but I was told I'm being held without bail."

Tessa felt the blood drain from her face. That was impossible. Then she realized once again, that money and power were doing the talking, just like in Tulsa. "Then God will find another way," she said with more confidence than she felt.

How Pastor could hear and pray out loud at the same time, she wasn't sure, but he vigorously nodded in agreement. "...and the sheriff of this fine county," he was saying, still in a loud voice. "Bless him every day as he works to keep peace in this area..."

"When you come again," Gaven said, "bring my overcoat. Take Erik over to the boarding house. My landlady will open up for him. Maybe you could bring a few of my school books as well."

"Of course. Anything else? I'm not sure what all they'll let you have." She jerked her head in the sheriff's direction. "He practically destroyed the cookies we brought."

"At least bring my Bible," he said.

At that, Pastor reached inside his coat and pulled out his small testament Bible and handed it through the bars, never missing a syllable of his prayer. Then laying his hand on Gaven's shoulder once again, he prayed for his protection and his soon release.

"That's enough of that noisy revival meeting in there," the sheriff hollered. "Time's up."

"I'll be back tomorrow," Tessa promised.

"And we'll bring you one of my coats," Pastor added.

"Come on outta there!" the sheriff hollered again.

Gaven placed a soft kiss into the palm of each of Tessa's hands. "Now don't worry about me. I was pinned down on the front lines in France once. This is nothing compared to that. Everything'll be fine. I love you, my darling little Tessa."

She nodded. "I love you too, Gaven."

Then Pastor was ushering her toward the door. As she looked back over her shoulder at him, she knew Gaven was putting on that brave smile just for her.

Chapter 15

Tessa knew she'd be unable to drive back to Pastor's house. Now that she'd actually seen Gaven locked up in that small dirty cage, she couldn't contain her tears.

As Pastor drove through the town of Sapulpa, he asked, "Do you know how to tell if you need more gasoline in this thing?"

Dabbing at her eyes with her hankie, she shook her head.

He pointed to a gauge. "This here's the one. Be sure to keep an eye on it." He drove up to a small general store where two tall skinny pumps stood sentinel out front. "And this gauge here tells you if it's overheating."

Tessa sniffed and wiped her nose. "What would I do if it overheated?"

"Put water in the radiator. I'll show you when we get back to the house. Always keep a container of water in the car."

A man in faded denim overalls emerged slowly from the store. "Nice car," he commented, studying the roadster.

"Thanks," Pastor answered, not volunteering any information.

The man peered in at them. "Fill 'er up?"

"Yes, please."

The smell of gasoline floated through the car as the tank was being filled.

"Can I get you a Nehi?" Pastor asked.

She opened her purse. "Let me see if I have anything."

He reached over and closed the purse. "Now Peanut, this is on me. The gasoline, too."

"I can't let you do that. You've already done so much."

"My pleasure," he said as he opened the door to get out. She watched as he opened the pop case which sat in front of the store, and pulled two dripping bottles of Nehi soda pop from the icy water. He popped the caps off using the opener on the side of the case and went inside.

As Tessa sat there waiting, she suddenly remembered how Gaven had not wanted to rent the apartment on Elwood. "Something" told him to wait a while. Had he perceived something was going to happen? Whatever it was, she knew there was wisdom in Gaven's decision and she was proud of him for making the right choice.

When Pastor came out from paying for the sodas and the gasoline, the screen door slammed loudly behind him. Although the day was still chilly, sunshine warmed the interior of the car, and the tangy orange soda tasted good and worked to clear the lump in her throat. Somehow she would pull herself together in order to help Gaven. But every time she thought of that cold cell, the tears came again.

On Saturday, they loaded everyone into the roadster to drive to Sapulpa. The great idea was thought up by quiet Siegrid. She kept asking to go along, but she was told they couldn't all go inside to see Gaven.

"Is there a window?" she wanted to know.

"There's a window in his cell with bars on it," Tessa remembered.

"Well then, if they won't let all of us in to see him, we can stand outside the window and he can at least look at us."

They were eating supper on Friday evening when she began this intense barrage. Once she brought up the idea, Vega quickly agreed. "I want to visit Gaven, too," she said. "And I know he wants to see us."

Pastor raised his white bushy brows. "They may have a point there."

Edith nodded. "Let's all go. It'll do him good to know we're all there, even if we can't go in."

So it was decided. The girls were thrilled to ride in Gaven's roadster.

Siegrid was right. Although the Sheriff Bynum was none too happy about the entire party converging on the jail, he couldn't stop them from going around to the back of the building and waving at Gaven. Even Siegrid was shouting and waving. Gaven stood on the cot to see out and was laughing and waving back. Tessa could tell their little party had infused him with fresh joy.

Mama and Edith had packed a lunch for Gaven with thick roast beef sandwiches on slices of homemade bread, and crisp apples from Edith's cellar. With Mama and Edith standing right there by the desk watching him, Sheriff Bynum didn't destroy the lunch, but he did look inside each sandwich.

After Mama learned how he mutilated the ginger cookies, she decided to make a batch just for the sheriff. It turned out to be a smart plan.

"I am told your favorite is ginger," she stated setting a box on his desk. The boots came down off the desk and hit the floor hard. He lifted off the lid and inhaled deeply. "For you they are," Mama said in her kindest voice.

"Why thank you kindly, ma'am. Not often I get any gifts in this job. Ever since my wife died a few years ago, I don't eat homemade cookies much."

"*Ya*. You have now whole box full of them."

Pastor brought Gaven a shaving kit as well as an overcoat of his. As Gaven placed the folded coat carefully on the cot, he said, "I'll be wrapped snug and warm in this tonight." To Tessa he said, "And the next time you come, this stubble will be gone." He rubbed at his chin.

But Tessa wouldn't have cared if he were clean shaven or not, she just wanted him out. It was harder than ever to say good-bye and leave him. The sheriff didn't yell quite so loudly this time and he let them visit an extra few minutes. Tessa couldn't bear to release Gaven's hands. Pastor gently took her by the shoulders and led her out.

THAT EVENING CLARETTE called. When Tessa was on the line, Clarette asked, "Is this a party line?"

Tessa answered that it was. "Four other families share this phone line."

"Then all I'll say is that I have some good news. Erik and I plan to drive down to Tulsa tomorrow to talk to you."

Tessa gave them the Walsh's address on Norfolk. "Thank you for your help, Clarette. It'll be so good to see you again. I only wish the circumstances could be different."

"Wait a minute, Tessa. Erik's asking about the bail. What was it set for?"

"There's no bail, Clarette. Tell him Gaven's being held without bail."

When Clarette repeated it to Erik, Tessa could hear her cousin roaring in the background. She knew how he felt.

"He says that's impossible," Clarette told her. "That is, among other things, that's what he said. We'll see you tomorrow and then we'll talk."

Knowing Clarette and Erik were planning to come to Tulsa on Sunday gave Tessa the needed impetus to leave. Everything inside her wanted to stay right there at Pastor's so she could go see Gaven every single day. As she loaded the car the next morning, it felt as though she were deserting him.

"We'll go over to the jail as often as we can this week," Pastor promised. But even that promise couldn't quiet the anxiety burning inside her.

As she drove the long lonely stretch of road from Pastor's house to the Glenn Pool, and then on to Tulsa she thrashed about in her mind of what to do next. She couldn't afford to drive down every weekend. And many times she had to work on Saturday. That plus the fact that bad weather could hit at any time, and she didn't relish the idea of driving this road in rain or snow all by herself. And yet how could she get through these days without him—knowing he was locked up in that horrid filthy cage? When she arrived at the Walsh's house, they were still at church. As she took her bag to her room, a sudden wave of weariness washed over her. She'd not slept well for the past two nights. Now all she wanted was to crawl into bed, pull up the covers and sleep. And she did—without even undressing.

The next thing she knew, Mina was there gently waking her. "Tessa. Tessa wake up. Your cousin and his wife are here."

Her sleep had been so heavy, and filled with visions of Gaven locked in jail. Now, she couldn't seem to rouse herself, as though she were in a drunken stupor.

"We're so glad you're safely home," Mina was saying. "How are you feeling? You look bushed. I'll get a cool cloth for you."

Tessa struggled to sit up as she heard Mina running water in the bathroom. Directly, she returned with a washcloth. Tessa pressed its coolness to her face and it did help to wake her.

"Can I get you something?"

She was being so sweet, but Tessa wanted nothing except for Gaven to be returned to her quickly and safely. "No. Nothing," she managed to say. "Just give me a minute to get myself together. I'll be right down."

Mina nodded and left. Tessa could hear the low rumble of conversation downstairs. She put on a fresh dress and brushed back her long hair, fastening it at the nape of her neck. Rinsing her face with cool water in the bathroom, she kept reminding herself that Clarette had said they were coming with good news. A cold north wind had whipped up creating a chill in the air, so she pulled on a sweater and went down.

They were all gathered in the kitchen where Mina had spread out cookies and a chocolate layer cake, along with the hot coffee. Clarette and Erik both jumped up the moment she entered the room. Concern etched their faces.

Tessa had almost forgotten how beautiful Clarette was, with her dark bobbed wavy hair, turned up nose and pretty pointed chin. She wasn't surprised that Shelby Harland had fallen hopelessly in love with the New York native. They ushered her to a chair, and of course everyone wanted to know how Gaven was faring.

It was impossible to explain the situation and remain dry-eyed. Pauline went to fetch Tessa a clean handkerchief. She told about both visits, about the sheriff and the short abbreviated visiting time. For the benefit of Clarette and Erik, she also had to re-tell the event when Hod tried to stop their truck. Erik was obviously fighting to control his anger. He kept shaking his head in disbelief as she talked.

"Are you sure it was gunshot you heard?" he said as she stopped to wipe tears from her eyes.

"I believe I know gunshots when I hear them. And if I don't, Gaven sure enough does," she said. "They may not have been firing directly at us, but they were shooting. If the truck hadn't caught in a rut, we would have gotten away and never even touched Hod."

"Do you think he was hurt badly?" Clarette wanted to know.

Tessa shrugged. "I heard the thud as the truck hit him and saw him fall away. Then Gaven told me to get down."

"It was obviously a trap," Russ said. His eyes, which usually twinkled with merriment, grew serious.

"No doubt about it," Erik agreed. "I don't guess Latham showed his face while you were there?"

Tessa shook her head. "At least I didn't see him. Who knows where he might be hiding. He's like a snake under a rock."

"A fit description," Erik said, taking a sip from his coffee mug. "Now tell me what's this nonsense about being held with no bail?"

"All I know is what Gaven told Pastor and me. That it was decided Gaven was to be held without bail."

Erik huffed and fumed. "That's the most ridiculous thing I've ever heard of. A travesty of justice and worse. We'll get an attorney and fight that one for sure. I'll talk to Dad about it as soon as we get home. He's always working through the system to assist his Indian friends, so I'm sure he can help on this as well."

"But he works mostly in Osage County," Clarette remarked. "What pull would he have in Creek Country?"

"I don't know, but surely he knows someone he can talk to."

"So what do I do now?" Tessa asked. She turned to her cousin. "What was the good news you had?" The more they talked the worse she felt. Just sitting around talking was doing no good at all.

"Clarette here made the call to New York," Erik said deferring to his wife.

"Your attorney friend's idea to call a federal agent was brilliant," Clarette told them. "There's one agent in New York whose reputation is sterling. Not only is he effective, but no one had ever bought him off. His name is Izzy Eisenbaum. This man is a master of disguises. He's fooled some of the best."

Clarette handed Tessa a slip of paper. "Give this name and number to the attorney, and have him make the connection. I was led to believe Izzy would be willing to take the first train out, but he needs more details first."

Tessa studied the writing on the paper. A federal agent coming all the way from New York? This was becoming very complicated. "What kind of details?"

"Legal jargon, I'm sure. Oh he did ask one thing. Is there anyone who knows where the still is located?"

Tessa hesitated a long moment. "I know."

Erik's blue eyes narrowed. "You've been to your Papa's stills?"

She nodded. "Both Berg and I went up there a few times when we were smaller."

"And you know the way?" Clarette asked.

"I know the way."

"It may have been moved by this time," Erik countered.

Tessa shook her head. "No need to move it when it's so well hidden."

Erik stood to his feet as though he could no longer handle the intensity of the moment. To Clarette he said, "What do you say we take Tessa over to Greenwood ourselves to deliver this message to the attorney."

"I'd like that," Clarette agreed. "I'd love to see Mama Sue again. Tessa? What do you say?"

It was Mina who then intervened. Putting her hand gently on Tessa's arm, she said, "I think Tessa's exhausted. Could you take the agent's name to the attorney without Tessa going along?"

Tessa felt wave of relief wash over her. She didn't have the strength to describe that jail cell one more time today.

"How unkind of us, Erik," Clarette said. "We just weren't thinking. Of course, we can do it. You stay here and rest, Tessa. We'll make our stop in Greenwood, then drive on back to Bartlesville." She pulled a notebook from her handbag and copied the name and number of the agent. "You keep that copy, Tessa—just in case."

"If you go to Mama Sue's house she'll tell you where to find Miles Calbert. He's been working out of the basement of the church, but since it's Sunday, I'm not sure where he'll be." Then Tessa remembered. "One other thing, Erik. Will you go to Gaven's room at the boarding house? He needs his overcoat, his Bible and some of his teacher's books."

"We can do that on the way to Greenwood." He looked at Clarette and she nodded her approval.

"We'll bring them back by here before leaving town."

Mina brought their coats from the hall closet. Graciously, Clarette thanked Mina for her hospitality.

Erik came to Tessa and put his big arm around her shoulder. "We'll not rest until he's out of there, Tessa. We'll do whatever it takes."

She thanked him, and thanked them both for coming. "If the agent does come here to Oklahoma, what then?" she asked.

"We'll have to wait and see," Clarette said, "but it seems there's enough evidence to lock up this Latham guy and get him out of the way."

Tessa still had dozens more questions, but few of them had answers. After they were gone, Mina tried to talk Tessa into eating supper, but she couldn't force herself to eat. She drank a glass of milk then went up to bed. The sharp wind blew about the house as she changed into her nightgown. She lay there in the semi-darkness thinking about Gaven in the cold cell with the north wind beating against it.

In all their talk that afternoon, no one spoke of that which she feared the most. The fact that the Klan could, in a matter of a few minutes, attack the small jail and overpower the ginger-cookie-loving Sheriff Bynum.

Sleep was a long time coming.

Chapter 16

Dragging out of bed Monday morning was something akin to pushing a trolley down Elgin Street. The moment Tessa awakened, Gaven was on her mind and the weight of it pushed her deeper into the softness of the bed. Sleep meant she didn't have to think. She didn't have to face the reality of his being gone. Or to face the fact that he wouldn't be by to pick her up that evening. And that he wouldn't be there tomorrow either. Without Gaven, there was no reason to get up. At all. Ever.

Mustering all her strength she pushed back the warm covers and crawled out of bed, pulling on her warm robe and knitted slippers. The dormer windows were decorated in a delicate lacing of frost. Through a little peephole in the frost, she could see a skiff of snow had fallen in the night.

Later when she went down to breakfast, Mina attempted to cheer her up. Somehow it only seemed to make things worse. Pauline wasn't scheduled at the telephone office until afternoon, so she was sleeping in. Tessa would have to walk to the trolley stop alone in the cold. Russ had left for work about an hour before Tessa got up.

Mina had prepared biscuits and gravy. The stack of golden brown biscuits was a work of art. Tessa knew she'd have to try to eat at least one. She didn't want to worry Mina, nor did she want to drag her friend down into the morass she was experiencing.

"I sat down with Russ and ate two of these biscuits," Mina said, "but I sure could eat another right about now."

Tessa knew that Mina was actually saying, if she didn't eat, Tessa might not eat. Almost patronizing. As they ate, Mina talked of the visit from Clarette and Erik last evening, how beautiful Clarette was, how handsome Erik was, how kind they both were to come, how blessed Tessa was to have that kind of help. Tessa half-listened.

"Will you be driving Gaven's car to work this morning?" Mina asked.

This brought Tessa out of her stupor. She hadn't even considered such a thing. She'd never had an automobile at her disposal before. "I'm not sure." Should she use it, or save the gas for diving back down to see Gaven?

"You may want to drive it today," Mina suggested. "It's pretty cold out, and besides you can drive over to Greenwood after work to see if that attorney has contacted the federal agent."

Tessa nodded. It was as though she needed someone to think for her. Her muddled mind refused to cooperate. "That's a good idea, Mina. Thank you."

It was rather nice not having to bear the cold wind walking to the trolley. Tessa found herself wishing Pauline weren't working the night shift. She could have given her a ride. How she wished she could do something to repay the Walshes. Why was she always on the receiving end? She seemed to only cause problems for people wherever she went.

Later, when she pushed open the front door of Halliburton-Abbott, she suddenly realized that she might not even have a job. She'd left quite abruptly last Thursday. Had it only been last Thursday? It felt more like a lifetime ago. She supposed it best to stop by Mr. Osborn's office first to make sure she was still in good standing.

In the cloakroom, she was cornered by Floy who was dying to know what was going on. Tessa explained as briefly as possible. With Floy it was rather difficult to be brief, for she asked many questions. "Who would be shooting at you?" she wanted to know. "And why? What made Gaven hit a man and then run off and leave him? That doesn't sound like your Gaven. He seems like such a nice sort of fella."

"Please Floy," Tessa said, suddenly weak with weariness, "I can't tell you any more than that. Please don't ask."

Floy backed up a step or two. "Hey don't get upset with me. I'm just trying to help."

"I know." Tessa gave a deep sigh. "I'm sorry. I didn't mean to snap at you. I've been so distressed since this happened, I can hardly think straight."

Her friend mellowed then. "Poor kid. Want me to go to Mr. Osborn's office with you? I'd be glad to."

How confusing to have the people closest to her sound so condescending. First Mina, now Floy. She knew they meant well, but Tessa didn't know how to handle it. "Thank you, Floy, I'll be fine."

She took the elevator to fourth where the administrative offices were located. Mr. Osborn's secretary showed Tessa into his office. The tastefully decorated office was equipped with the latest typewriters and dictating machines—the picture of efficiency that their manager displayed both inside his office and out. While Mr. Osborn didn't seem to be angry with her, his nice toothpaste-ad smile was missing.

"I understand you simply walked off your job last week, Miss Jurgen."

"I received an emergency phone call giving me bad news about my fiancé. I wasn't thinking clearly. I'm sorry."

"We're not without compassion in the management of Halliburton-Abbott, but if an emergency arises, please come to me about it first."

"Yes sir. I will sir." At least she thought she would. At this point she was no longer sure of anything. With a mild warning, Mr. Osborn dismissed her.

Traffic in the store was slow. Tessa straightened the remnant table at least three times, reorganized the button and buckle displays, and straightened all the loops of embroidery threads. The clock on the wall mocked her as minutes refused to move. When a customer did come in, Tessa felt herself withdrawing into her shell, barely talking. She thought lunch time would never arrive. When it did, she retreated to the employee lounge and wrote Gaven a letter. Writing to him gave her at least a small semblance of connection to him.

On the first page, she told him about the visit from Erik and what Clarette had learned about the agent. Abruptly the thought hit her that his letters would be opened and read. Tearing the page from the tablet she ripped it to tiny pieces and dropped it in the trash basket. She'd have to be very careful in what she wrote, which made writing him even more difficult. She quickly wrote what she could to try to cheer him up and infuse hope into the situation. But she felt none of it.

The afternoon was a duplicate of the long slow morning, only worse—as though she were swimming through gelatin. A customer came in wanting four yards of wool plaid. Unthinking, Tessa measured and then cut only three yards. Just as the customer was complaining, Ila came strolling by jangling her keys and heard every word. She stepped in to rectify the situation. Flustered and upset, Tessa apologized profusely and was horribly embarrassed. When the customer was gone, Ila said, "That's an expensive error, Miss Jurgen. If it happens again, I'll be forced to delete the amount from your paycheck."

When quitting time finally arrived, Tessa fairly flew to fetch her coat and hat, and ran down the street to where she'd parked Gaven's car. After mailing his letter at the post office, she drove to Greenwood. Chloe would not be there, but she'd try to find Miles.

At the remains of the Mount Zion Church, Tessa saw Preacher Sam there in the cold, working on the cleanup. When the others could help, they did, but meanwhile, he continued to move every burned fragment by his own hands. In spite of his ample weight he could hold his own when it came to hard physical labor.

He greeted Tessa with a wide smile and a wave. "Miss Tessa," he called out. "Hullo there. You looking for Miles I suppose?"

"Is he here?" she asked as she stepped out of the car.

Preacher Sam pointed toward the basement. "Still down in his little cubbyhole." He came toward her, pulling off his leather glove and offering his hand. "We had a nice visit with Mister Erik and his lovely wife last evening. So good to see them again."

She nodded, not really wanting to chit chat.

"Come on," he said gently, as though reading her mind. "Let's go see what Miles got to say."

Miles sat hunched over a stack of law books spread out on his makeshift desk. He stood when Preacher Sam rapped on the door.

"Ah Miss Jurgen. I was hoping to see you today. I want you to know what's going on. Please sit down." He pulled up a straight-back wooden chair for her. "Visiting with your cousin and his wife last evening was a tremendous help. Thanks for sending them over."

"I would have come too, but..."

"Now there, Miss Tessa," Preacher Sam said, "no need for apologies. We know what you going through." And he truly did.

"I was finally able to reach this federal agent, named Izzy Eisenbaum, Mrs. Torsten told us about. I talked to his superior and it's true that he's not in debt to anyone. Mr. Izzy seems to like the idea coming way out West, as he calls it, and shutting down a moonshine still. He should be here by the end of the week."

End of the week. This was only Monday. Tessa feared for Gaven's safety meanwhile. "Is there something we can do to get him out on bail?" she asked.

Miles tapped a pencil on the open book in front of him. "From what I can make of this whole mess, they seem to be treating Mr. Gaven as though he were a black, or even a Jew."

"Or one of them union guys that the Klan don't like," Preacher Sam offered. "They strings them up just as quick as they do a black."

Miles nodded. "What Lanny and I think, is that this Hod Latham wants Mr. Gaven out of the way because of you. And the Klan is cooperating full force because of Mr. Gaven's involvement here—bringing us the lumber and all that. So it boils down to a two-way squeeze." He marked the place in the book with a scrap of paper, closed it and set it out of the way. "How active is Hod Latham in the Klan, Miss Tessa? Do you know?"

Tessa shook her head. "For the most part, Hod's always been a loner. All we know is that one of his bootlegging buddies was inducted as a Kleagle. Last winter Pastor Stedman told me that Hod's association with that kind of leadership might bring him into Tulsa."

"And did it?"

"It certainly did. He found me and that was the night Jasper and Strapper came along and saved my life. There was a terrible rainstorm, and..." The nightmare experience shook her even now, remembering how sinister Hod could be.

"He tried to kidnap you? Is that what you're saying?" Miles' voice was soft.

Tessa nodded. "I was fighting to get loose when the boys came up and Strapper grabbed Hod. Jasper led me racing through the alleyways to escape."

"There were no other witnesses? Other than the boys?"

"It was raining hard. No one was out."

Miles leaned back in his chair. "I wish we could get the guy for attempted kidnapping, but that would be a long shot."

"Strapper still be in hiding," Preacher Sam said. "Even if he come back to Tulsa, no white judge gonna believe him."

"You're right," Miles agreed.

Tessa appreciated Miles trying to get to the bottom of everything, but she was becoming frustrated. "Where does that leave us? Can't we get an attorney to help us?" Even as she said it, she was embarrassed. What she had really said was, "Can't we get a *white* attorney to help us." Obviously Miles was doing all he could, but his hands were tied. "I'm sorry," she added quickly. "I didn't mean to seem ungrateful."

"No need to be sorry, Miss Tessa," Preacher Sam said with a smile. "We knows we got limits in helping. But like the Bible say, 'can the leopard change his spots?'" Then chuckled at his own joke.

"You could find another attorney," Miles said, "but in the climate around here just now, it'd be somewhat risky. I'm not sure how you could find out for sure who's on whose side."

She knew he was right. "So what do we do?"

"I feel confident about this agent coming. My advice is that we wait for him and let him move in on Hod Latham."

The long days of that week stretched out in front of her. Endless days of not knowing. Even after the agent arrived, there was no promise... She felt her shoulders slump.

"What say you come on over to see Mama Sue 'fore you go home." Preacher Sam was on his feet. "She be mighty glad to see you."

Tessa reached out to shake Miles' hand. "Thank you for all you've done. I appreciate it more than you'll ever know."

"Wish it could be more." Miles waved at the law books. "Meanwhile I'll keep digging. Who knows what I might come up with?"

It was growing dark, and Tessa needed to get on home, but she wanted to see Mama Sue for a few minutes. She gave Preacher Sam a lift the few blocks through the twilight to his house. Mama Sue was standing at the back steps when they arrived. "I thought that sounded like Mr. Gaven's car out there. It don't chug like no Model T. Nice sounding car."

Tessa was given a big hug as she entered the kitchen. "Any chance of you staying for supper?"

"The Walshes are expecting me."

"Then let's say a prayer together for Mr. Gaven. We already been doing a heap of praying for that boy."

She led Tessa to sit at the kitchen table where she and Preacher Sam both began to pray out loud, separate, but in unison. The effect was glorious. She could feel her spirit being revived.

Once they both "amen-ed," Mama Sue took Tessa's hands and looked square into her eyes. "You be strengthened by the Lord. Go in His strength; not yours."

"I have none. None at all," Tessa admitted.

"Good. That means you rely totally on Him!"

Tessa found herself repeating those words over to herself many times in the coming days. "I'm relying on you, Lord. Totally on you."

Another skiff of snow fell through the night and the north wind blew mercilessly all through Tuesday. Again Tessa wrote a letter to Gaven during her lunch hour and mailed it after work. She didn't drive Gaven's car that day. Somehow it didn't seem right to drive it only for her own comfort.

The raw wind pummeled her all the way from the trolley stop to the Walsh's front door step. In spite of being wrapped in the warm muffler Mama had knitted, her face was numb from the icy cold. The warmth of the living room awakened every frozen part causing her fingers and toes to tingle and burn. How was Gaven faring through this terrible cold spell?

She hung her coat and hat in the hall closet and went to the kitchen where Mina was busy with supper preparations. "Tessa, there's a letter for you on the hall table."

"From Gaven?" She felt her insides leap.

"No, from the university. Very official-looking."

The university. In all that had happened, she'd almost forgotten. All else had been overshadowed by Gaven's arrest. She moved to the hallway and picked up the letter. It was indeed quite official-looking. She tore open the envelope, pulled out the one-page letter and unfolded it. Her eyes blurred as she tried to focus the cold, black words on the paper:

Dear Miss Jurgen: We regret to inform you that your application for admission to Tulsa University has failed to be accepted by our board.

Chapter 17

Tessa grabbed tightly to the heavy walnut table to keep from falling. It couldn't be. She knew her scores were high. There must be some mistake. But her tired mind couldn't fight this battle on top of the one with Gaven.

Mina stepped from the kitchen into the hall. "What is it, Tessa? Tessa?" Mina hurried to Tessa's side. "You're pale as you can be."

"They don't want me, Mina." She handed the letter over.

"I can't believe this." Mina stared at the letter in disbelief. "Why, it doesn't even say anything about the scholarship—just that you weren't accepted. This makes no sense. Absolutely no sense at all. Wait till Russ sees this."

"Oh, please, Mina. Let's not bother everyone with more of my problems. I can't bear it."

"But maybe he can help."

"I'm so tired of needing help from everyone." Tessa pulled away from Mina's grasp and ran for the stairs. "There's nothing anyone can do. Nothing." Like a child, she ran to her room and closed the door, flinging herself across the bed sobbing.

She was grateful Mina didn't follow. Eventually she cried herself to sleep. When she awakened, she was chilled. The alarm clock on her dresser said nine-thirty. She'd slept the entire evening away. Taking her warm sweater from her closet, she pulled it on and went downstairs. She owed them all an apology.

They were in the living room where Pauline was working a jigsaw puzzle, Russ was reading the paper, and Mina sat with her embroidery in her lap.

"Hello everyone."

"Oh Tessa, there you are." Mina started to get up.

"Please. Sit still. I just wanted to apologize to you. All three of you. You've been so kind through all of this, and I've been wallowing in so much self-pity, I'm not much good for anything."

"Nobody blames you," Pauline said. "I'd be the same way and worse."

"Thank you." Tessa sat down on the low hassock. "I've made up my mind, I can't just sit around here moping. I'm going to pack my things and go stay with Pastor and Edith until Gaven is released."

"Are you sure that's what's best?" Mina said. "You could lose your job."

"I've thought of that, but I don't care. I knew the moment I awakened a few moments ago what I should do. And since I've made that decision, I feel stronger. My mind is clearer."

"What about the university?" Pauline wanted to know. "Do you think they made a mistake? Maybe they mixed up the test scores or something."

"I can't even think about that now. All that matters is Gaven, and I've got to be there." She stood to her feet. "May I use the phone? I need to call Mr. Osborn."

"What about this federal agent who's coming into Tulsa?" Russ asked, folding his newspaper.

"I've thought of that. I'll leave a map with you showing how to get to Pastor's house. That agent will have to come down there anyway if he has any hopes of finding Hod. I can have Miles direct him to your house. His name is Izzy Eisenbaum."

Now that she had a plan Tessa felt totally different. As she expected, Mr. Osborn said he couldn't promise she'd have a job when she returned. She told him she understood. "God provided me this job, surely He's big enough to find me another," she said.

Snow lay about the hills as she drove to the Glenn Pool the next morning, but the roads were clear. The ruts were frozen hard and the ride was tortuously bumpy. In the back were her bags and a few of Gaven's things, which Erik had gathered up for her.

She'd been putting away a little money each week, hoping to purchase a few things for her wedding. But now she would use it for purchasing the gasoline needed to drive back and forth to see Gaven. Weather permitting, she'd go every day. Thanksgiving was coming, and she'd make sure Gaven had his Thanksgiving dinner even if she had to hand it through the bars piece by piece.

Pastor was out visiting his parishioners when she arrived, and the girls were in school. Mama and Edith were both pleased she'd decided to stay for a while. After unloading her bags, Tessa announced she was heading out for Sapulpa.

"Don't go without Royce with you," Edith said. "It's just not safe."

"How long will he be gone?"

"I can find him right quick, now that there's a telephone in this house." She hurried to the box phone hanging on the kitchen wall and ground the ringer around a couple of times. "Irma? This is Edith Stedman. I'm looking for Pastor. Would you start calling a few places to see if we can find him?" Edith glanced at Tessa and gave a wink. "Just tell him to call home. We have company."

Tessa didn't have long to wait. Before Edith could pour her a cup of hot cider, the wall phone sang out two longs and a short, which was the Stedmans' party line ring. "You catch it, Tessa, and surprise him."

It was Pastor and he was ecstatic to hear her voice. "I kept telling everyone I thought you should be here."

"You think I did the right thing? I may not have a job when I go back."

"The Lord's guiding you, Peanut. Plenty of jobs in Tulsa, but only one Gaven. You hang tight now. I'll be there in two shakes of a lamb's tail."

Edith and Mama had insisted that Pastor take Gaven a change of clothes so they could clean and launder what he'd been wearing.

Now Mama fetched the package with his clean things wrapped inside. "These the pastor was to take to Gaven today. Now you vill take them. Better you give to him than Pastor." She smiled as she spoke, then gave Tessa a gentle kiss on her cheek.

As Tessa took the clean, freshly pressed clothes and placed them in the back of the roadster, she realized that even Mama was pleased at her decision to come home for a time. Presently she heard Pastor's Model T rumbling up the road. It took him only a jiffy to take in the crate of eggs and gallon of milk, gifts from one of their church members. She was happy to have him drive. Her legs were still tired from the rough drive from Tulsa.

No one was as happy to see her as Gaven. Mama made sure Tessa went armed with a box of ginger cookies for Sheriff Bynum. The cookies magically made each visit last a little longer.

Gaven was dressed in some of Pastor's too-large clothes, but he was clean-shaven and looked wonderful to Tessa. She wanted nothing more than to stand and gaze at him.

"It's only Wednesday," he said with a wide grin. "Did Halliburton-Abbott change their store hours?"

"I may not be working there any longer," she told him. "But it doesn't matter. I packed my things to stay with Pastor and Edith until you get out of here."

Releasing one of her hands, he pressed the back of his hand to his face to stop a tear. "Thank you, my darling. I confess I need you here. Desperately."

"I'm here. I'll be here every day."

"I told you the other day that I'd been through worse than this in the war." He gave a wry smile as he patted her hand. "But now I realize that during the war I wasn't missing a beautiful girl who had become a special part of my life."

"You got quite a little firecracker there," Pastor said. "And look what she brought you. Your books!"

Gaven's eyes lit up as the sight of his teacher's books. "I'll never complain about needing to study ever again. I'm starved for those books."

Pastor fit them through the bars one by one.

"Remember that regal tiger we saw at the zoo, Tessa?" Gaven asked.

Tessa remembered because they had shared a special kiss in front of that tiger's cage.

"The longer I'm in here, the more of an affinity I feel with that poor caged animal. I've practically worn out this floor with my pacing."

"That tiger may have a life sentence," she retorted, "but we're getting you out of here soon. Pastor, will you pray for us?" She gave a wink. On cue, Pastor moved nearer the door and prayed a boisterous prayer as Tessa explained to Gaven about the agent who was to arrive at the end of the week. Then she told him what Miles said about the Klan and their possible involvement. But Gaven had already come to that conclusion.

"I asked if we should get an attorney, but he suggested we wait and let this agent do his stuff first."

Gaven nodded. "That makes sense, but it's agony having to wait."

It was agony for Tessa, too. But her agony was in knowing it was because of her that he was sitting in that cold cage.

That evening they all sat in the parlor together. The girls pronounced spelling words to one another. Edith's crochet needle was creating a little white pillow cover on which Tessa's ring would be carried in the wedding. Mama sewed another dozen or so tiny pearls on the dress.

Pastor's gray head was bent over his papers and Bible at the desk. Every once in a while, he would mutter something that he had discovered, then scratch a few more notes in his sermon notebook.

Tessa had started knitting Gaven a dark blue muffler. The soft yarn and the clicking needles felt good in her hands. As the piece grew longer she imagined the look on his face when she gave it to him. It would be a Christmas gift, she told herself resolutely.

———— ◉ ————

THE RINGING TELEPHONE in the kitchen broke into the quiet. Edith went to the kitchen to answer, and came back into the parlor with a puzzled expression. "It's for you, Tessa. Long distance from Mrs. MacIntyre."

"*Mrs.* MacIntyre. Gaven's mother? Calling here? How..."

"No matter," Mama chided, shooing at Tessa with her hands. "Go. Go. Talk to her."

"What shall I tell her?"

"How about the truth?" Pastor said looking up from his Bible.

Tessa walked slowly into the kitchen and took the receiver from where Edith left it on top the phone. "Hello?"

"Tessa? Tessa Jurgen?"

"Yes."

"I apologize for bothering you. You're Gaven's fiancé, are you not?" There was a distinct British accent over the crackling lines.

"I am."

"Your name was given me at Gaven's boarding house. Then I called the number of a family named Walsh and they gave me this number. I'm sorry to be such a bother, but I'm terribly worried about Gaven. I've not heard from him for several days. It's not like him not to call or write."

"We should have called you, Mrs. MacIntyre, I'm sorry. You see, there was a kind of an accident."

"Accident? Gaven? Is he hurt?"

"No, no. He's fine. That is..." Tessa's mind was a jumble. She had no idea where to start. "Gaven's in jail right now, but he didn't do anything wrong."

"Jail?" Panic rose up in her voice. "How dreadful. I knew terrible things would happen if he stayed in that wild country out there. I wanted him to come home to Pennsylvania with his father and me, but he refused. Now this."

"We're doing everything we can to get him freed. I'll tell him you called and that he should write you a letter right away explaining everything. He can explain it much better than I can." Tessa was practically shouting. Sharp static and loud crackling on the line made talking close to impossible.

"What are the charges?" Mrs. MacIntyre wanted to know.

Tessa tried to explain about the ambush at Lone Grove Crossroads and the accident with Hod, but the static overpowered her words.

"I can hardly hear you," Gaven's mother said. "Please have him write to me. Tell him that Mother said for him to cease all this silly hero business. The war was quite enough."

"Yes, I'll tell him, Mrs. MacIntyre." And the line went dead.

Tessa went back to the parlor and took up her knitting. "What an awful way to meet my future mother-in-law," she said.

Later, Mama brought the stunning lace-covered wedding dress over to where Tessa was sitting. "You are here; Gaven is not. Mark the hem, ve can now. Downstairs in the warmth."

"Good idea, Gerta," Edith agreed. "Just step inside the kitchen and slip it on, Tessa."

Tessa touched the cool silky satin as she pulled the dress up over her shoulders. Siegrid and Vega oohed and aahed over the beauty of the dress, gazing at her in wonderment as Tessa returned to the parlor. The phone call from Gaven's mother continued to plague her. What must she think of this girl who was dragging her son into so much trouble? The other question which gnawed at her like a rat in the grain bin—what if Gaven were brought to trial and convicted? What then? Would there even be a wedding? Ever? The exquisite dress seemed to mock her and all her previous excitement simply melted away.

—————◉—————

ON HER NEXT VISIT TO the jail, she told Gaven about the call from his mother.

He smiled. "Did she say I should be living in Pennsylvania where it's safer?"

"Something like that."

"I'll get a letter to her today. I promise." Then more gently, "I hope the call didn't upset you."

"I'm sure it was much more upsetting to her."

—————◉—————

WITH EACH PASSING DAY, Tessa felt it more and more unlikely that a mob would come after Gaven. If the Klan had planned that ploy, they no doubt would have done it quickly. Perhaps their tactic was to simply let the system take its course. Putting him in prison might be their aim.

On Friday, when she and pastor arrived back home from their daily trip to the jail, Edith said there'd been a call from Miles Calbert. "He said to tell you a visitor from New York has arrived in Tulsa and he's heading this way. Should be here this evening." She reached out to help Tessa out of her coat which was dusted lightly with snow. "He was very cautious in the way he talked."

"He knows to be careful. Did he say anything about the map at the Walsh's?" Tessa asked.

"He just said to tell you everything was being taken care of."

After supper, they sat quietly in the parlor waiting. Even the girls were quiet and subdued. They attempted to work on their lessons, but kept whispering about the man from New York City. The most they knew about New York was that it was further away than Tulsa.

When the motorcar drove up out front, each of them jumped. The girls started for the front door first, but Mama stopped them with a stern look. "Sit quiet," she said softly.

Pastor answered the knock at the door.

Tessa wasn't sure what she had expected. Perhaps a tall suave well-dressed dapper gentleman. But Izzy Eisenbaum was none of that. He was short and nearly as wide as he was high, but as Pastor politely took his coat, Tessa could see it was mostly muscle.

"Did the snow cause any problems?" Pastor asked after welcoming the stranger.

"You call this snow? You want snow you should come to New York. I show you snow. Up past yer neck almost." His round face was open and cheery almost like a child's, and his words came at a fast clip. He popped open a leather wallet in which Tessa could see a shiny government badge. After Pastor looked at it and nodded, Izzy slipped it back into his pocket. He rubbed his hands together and blew on them to warm them. "Can't say much for that old car out there." He jerked his thumb toward the door. "No heater. Liked to froze."

Pastor introduced him all round, then Edith and Mama went to the kitchen to prepare spiced cider and donuts.

Izzy settled his short frame onto the horsehair sofa and looked around the room appreciatively.

"Always wanted to travel out West. Now here I am. Nice." He nodded as though giving his stamp of approval. "Nice."

When Edith served the cider he sniffed at it and joked about what might be in it. The girls sat and stared at him.

"I got girls about youse girls ages," he said, chomping down on a donut. He made "girls" sound like "goils." Tessa was fascinated.

Once he had devoured about four donuts, he was ready to get down to business. He pulled a pad and pencil from his coat pocket and began asking Tessa question after question. He wanted all the background information she could give on Hod Latham. She fished back into her memories attempting to remember all she could about his operation and how her father had helped in it.

Izzy also wanted to know all about her involvement in the riot and what she knew about Klan activities. There wasn't much she could tell, but she shared what she knew.

"And this here moonshiner, Latham, is in cahoots with the Klan?"

"Word has it," Pastor put in, "that one of his bootlegging buddies is a Kleagle."

"Is that right?" Izzy's stubby fingers scribbled notes. "Seems kinda odd since the Klan's been singing the praises of prohibition and claims to be a dry bunch. And they say politics makes strange bedfellows."

"And what is prohibition if not purely political?" Pastor quipped, which set the short little man to laughing.

"Ya gotta point there, Reverend. Now I need to ask the little lady something. That Tulsa attorney, Cal... What's his name?"

"Miles Calbert."

"Yeah, that one. He says that this Latham guy with all the hootch up in the hills is sorta sweet on you. What's the deal here?"

As clearly as she could, she explained to him the incident of her father making some kind of deal with Hod, with her as the payoff.

Izzy shook his head. "Strange kind of father, if you don't mind me saying so. Where's this father of yours now?"

"Her father's dead," Pastor Stedman answered for her.

"In a raid? Or did one of his chumps do him in?"

"We need to tell him everything, Pastor," Tessa said. "To answer your question Mr. Eisenbaum, my father was murdered in some kind of argument about one of his bootlegging deals. They say the man shot in self-defense."

"Figures." He scribbled more notes, then glanced over at Mama. "I don't mean no offense, ma'am."

Mama's face showed some of the strain she was feeling in all these strange goings on. However, she gave a slight smile and nodded.

"One more thing," Izzy said, "Am I right that this Hod guy is still thinking he's got dibs on you?"

"Dibs?"

"Yeah, dibs. Like he's got rights."

Tessa nodded. "Very much so."

"Okay." He closed his notebook as though everything had been taken care of, then stood up.

"You're welcome to stay here for the night," Pastor told him. "It's late and the weather's bound to get worse."

"Naw. I got me a room over in Sapulpa. Gotta case the joint and see what's going on over there."

"What are you going to do, Mr. Eisenbaum?" Tessa wanted to know. She thought there'd be more answers than this.

"First I'm gonna de-fuse that noisy Klan. They're gonna have to start talking straighter. If they're dry, they're dry. I'll talk with some of the stiffs who run the show. Get them to drop this Hod fella like a hot potato."

"How will you know where to find them?" Pastor asked.

Izzy grinned as he pulled on his heavy wool overcoat and firmed his hat on. "A guy can get in just about anywhere if you know how." He jabbed his thumb at his chest. "I happen to know how. Once we get the guard dogs shut down, then we close in on the moonshiner."

Turning to Tessa he said. "I'm right in supposing you'll help us get him." It was a statement not a question. "I mean, you want your sweetheart outta the clink, right?"

Tessa could only nod.

"If this moonshiner is as secluded as you say, and you're tasty bait..." Turning to Pastor he said, "Pardon me, Reverend." Then to Tessa, "It's pretty clear to me that you're the one thing he'll let down his guard for. Once he's out of the way, there's no one to press charges. Poof."

A shiver ran up Tessa's spine. "What will I need to do?"

"Can you get word to Latham that you wanna talk?"

Tessa glanced at Pastor Stedman.

"We can get word to him," Pastor said solemnly.

"That's all I need to know for now. I'll be in touch."

And like a little gremlin, he vanished into the snowy night.

Chapter 18

When Gaven heard the gist of Eisenbaum's plan during Tessa's visit on Saturday, he was dead set against it. "It's too dangerous, Tessa. Latham's crazy. He could do something so quick..."

"But I won't be alone. Just a decoy. If there were another way, I'm sure Mr. Eisenbaum would do it. From what Clarette tells me, he knows what he's doing."

Gaven leaned heavily onto the bars of the cell, shaking his head. "I can't let you put yourself in that kind of danger."

Tessa gently reached up to touch his cheek. "It's because of me that you're in here. I'm willing to do what's necessary to get you out."

"None of this is your fault," he countered. "You aren't responsible for the actions of a mad man."

"Mr. Eisenbaum says the first step is to call off the guard dogs, as he calls the Klan. Without their backing, Hod won't be so dangerous."

Silence hung between them for a moment. Pastor Stedman was in the outer room carrying on a lively conversation with the Sheriff. "Another few visits," Pastor had said earlier that morning, "and we'll have that Sheriff ready to go to heaven."

Presently, Gaven said, "Promise me one thing."

"If I can."

"Before you agree to anything, get Erik down here to be with you."

"But he has a newspaper to get out every week."

"He'll come. Promise me you'll call him."

She hated to bring yet another person in this mess. But how could she refuse Gaven? "All right I'll call him."

SHE DIDN'T HAVE LONG to think about her promise. Izzy was back at the house that very evening. After Siegrid and Vega were put to bed, he explained how he had approached the Oklahoma Klavern leaders and convinced them to revoke the membership of Hod and any of his bootlegging cronies. "I hadda remind them of their own burning of stills."

"What was the answer?" Tessa marveled that this man would know right where to go to find a Klan Imperial Wizard. How frightening that would be.

"Aw they just said he slipped by their noses. You know how it is—when membership is ten bucks and another six for a sheet and a hood, anyone gets in."

Pastor was leaning forward in the wingback chair, his hands cupped around his coffee mug. "Without their backing, doesn't that mean there's no case against Gaven? Can't he just go free?"

"You just want the nice guy sprung? Or do you wanna get rid of the real problem?"

Tessa spoke up. "We want to take care of the real problem,"

"But Tessa..." Pastor started.

"This seems to be our chance to put Hod away, Pastor. What chance will we have after Mr. Eisenbaum leaves?" Like Gaven, Pastor wanted to spare her from having to go through with this, but there was no choice.

"The chick's right, Reverend."

"Animals when cornered," Mama said softly, "more dangerous they become. A man vill be the same."

"Armed agents will be right behind her," Izzy assured her. Turning back to Tessa, he said. "That roadster sitting out there—it belongs to your boyfriend?"

"Yes, that's Gaven's car."

"Can you drive it right to Latham's moonshine setup?"

Tessa remembered riding the back roads with her father in the buckboard pulled by their two mules. That was in good weather. Now there was snow on the ground, and she'd only been driving a short time. Then she thought of Gaven sitting in that jail cell and Hod's desperate attempt to get rid of him.

She nodded. "I can do whatever it takes."

"That's a girl." Izzy helped himself to another one of Mama's fluffy cinnamon rolls. "Get word to Latham that you're ready to talk to him about getting MacIntyre set free. Hopefully, he'll think you're giving yourself over in exchange for his release. This should make Latham more willing to see you."

"What if he wants to meet me at another place?"

"You set the meeting place. Don't give options."

Tessa took a deep breath. Pastor was giving her a nod. "Just tell us when," she said.

"I won't be coming by again. Even though I've changed automobiles twice, it's still risky. No telling who sees what around here." The short man stood to his feet and stretched. "We'll get word to you letting you know the time."

After he left, Tessa fulfilled her promise to call Erik, explaining only briefly that Gaven asked her to have him come. Due to the party line, she remained vague as to the details.

"Gaven insisted I call to let you know," she explained.

"Dad's in town this week," Erik said. "He can put out the paper for us. Clarette and I will drive down there first thing in the morning."

She gave him directions to Pastor's house and rang off.

⟞⟝

TESSA HAD LOOKED FORWARD all week to Sunday, when she could once again enjoy one of Pastor's sermons in their little community church. She was surrounded by loving friends and neighbors who were excited that she'd come back for a visit. She was careful how she answered questions, and gave out as little information as possible.

On Sunday afternoon, the Stedman house was even fuller with the arrival of Erik and Clarette. Siegrid and Vega were all agog over Clarette's New York wardrobe. The first thing Erik wanted to do, of course, was to go see Gaven, but Pastor cautioned against it. "My advice is for all of us to sit tight until Izzy Eisenbaum has a chance to work his little plan."

If the situation hadn't been so grave, and if Gaven had been with them, the time would have been like a holiday. Erik hadn't seen his Aunt Gerda for years and they sat together at the kitchen table talking while Erik filled her in on all the latest family news.

On Monday morning, a furniture store delivery truck appeared in the Stedman driveway. A man dressed like a delivery driver came to the front door and asked for Pastor. He handed him a note and left. The note indicated they were to get word to Hod Latham that she would meet him at his moonshine still sometime in the afternoon on Tuesday.

Presently, Pastor left in his Model T to make the connection with someone who would get word to Hod. Tessa had no idea who it was, nor did she want to know.

Through that night Tessa tossed and turned as sleep fled. Images of Hod's face and exploding gunfire harassed her mind. Over and over she told herself it didn't matter what happened to her. The agents would be there, and Hod would be taken in—dead or alive. Then Gaven would go free.

When she came downstairs before daylight the next morning, Mama was in the kitchen sorting through a barrel of old clothes.

"Whatever are you doing?" she asked. Then she recognized one of Berg's old shirts. "Those are Berg's clothes! You still have them?"

"When the men they come to move us, I vant to throw things away. Pastor he says, 'No Gerta. Not now. Pack them. Bring them. Put them in our shed.' So I do that." She held up a pair of wool trousers. "These you wear to stay warm. Just in case. Should the car be stuck in snow, you may walk."

Gingerly Tessa picked up a worn flannel shirt and held it to her face. What a wise mother she had. And what a joy it would be to be bundled in Berg's clothes.

Tessa had no desire for food. Even though Mama and Edith put out a large spread for both breakfast and lunch, she could eat little.

Shortly after lunch she went up to her room and dressed in two layers of Berg's clothes. Beneath the shirts she fastened on her strand of pearls. Whatever happened, she wanted to be wearing them.

The roadster was parked near the back door. Pastor brought out a pair of his galoshes and placed them in the car. "You never know," he said.

Then there was Erik pulling on his heavy coat. "What are you doing?" she asked him.

"I'm going with you."

"But you can't, Erik. You'll spoil everything. Izzy didn't say..."

Erik placed his large hands on her shoulders. "Now Tessa, why do you think Gaven had you call me? I know him. He wanted me to be with you. I'll be right here on the floor in the back."

"But what about Clarette?" She looked helplessly at Erik's wife, but she just shrugged.

"I'm beginning to learn just how stubborn a Swede can be," she said with a smile. "He has to go. For you. For Gaven. For himself."

"I let you down last spring when you were crying for help," Erik said as he crawled into the back.

"But I'm not crying for help now," she protested.

"I shouldn't have to wait to hear the cry."

Looking at the little group, she could tell they were all relieved that Erik would be with her.

Pastor said a quick prayer and she was off.

Truth be known, she was terribly relieved to have Erik's presence in that back seat. He joked and chatted with her as he took the bumps bravely.

"Does Gaven ever talk about our war days?" he asked. His voice sounded like someone was beating him on his back.

"Not much. I've asked a few questions, but he doesn't seem to want to talk about it."

"That's because we all wanted to come home and forget. Me included. He told you we were with the ambulance corps, didn't he?"

"I knew that much."

"It wasn't easy driving to the front, picking up the wounded and taking them back to the hospitals. But we were a whole lot better off than those poor fellas in the trenches."

Tessa wondered why he was telling her this. Maybe he simply needed to talk.

"We still got shot at, and sometimes we'd get pinned down when the shelling started. Ouch! I felt that bump."

"Sorry. I can't figure out whether to stay in the ruts, or stay out of them."

"Same difference. Anyway, one day we were going to the front lines. Right up to where the trenches were. Thank goodness the ambulance was empty. All of a sudden there were explosions everywhere. I yelled at Gaven to bail out."

As he talked, they left the straight level rutted roads into curves and tree-studded hills. Thick stands of scrub oak lined either side as the road narrowed and became less defined.

"Where are we now?" he asked.

"Coming into the hills," she answered back, then waited a moment. "Is there more to your story?"

"I'm scootching around to get more comfortable. Where was I?"

"You bailed out of the ambulance..."

"Oh yeah. Well, Gaven he took out on a dead run, and I was right behind him. All of a sudden there was an explosion and everything went black. I didn't know what happened. Later I woke up down in a trench with Gaven beside me."

"What happened? Were you hurt?" She'd known none of this before.

"I'd been knocked silly, but not really hurt. The foot soldiers told me how Gaven had landed safe in the trench, but when he saw I wasn't right behind him, he scrambled back out to come and get me."

"Oh my goodness!"

"They tried to stop him, Tessa, but that guy wouldn't be stopped. He was coming after me no matter what. I'm a lot bigger than he is. Can you imagine him dragging my dead weight through that shelling?"

Tessa could imagine. Even though she hadn't known Gaven then, she felt the anguish of the moment as though it were happening that very second.

"Now you know why I'm riding back here today," he concluded. "I'd do anything for that guy. Even get bumped and bruised in the back of his old jalopy. Now where are we?"

"Our old cabin is just a few miles off the road to our right, if that tells you anything."

The roadster took the hills bravely, but she found herself fighting in places to keep it from slipping off in the snow.

"Have you caught sight of anyone following us?" Erik asked.

"No. No one." She tried to keep her voice steady. She dared not think that something might have stalled Izzy and his fellow agents. Clarette said they knew their business; Tessa had to trust that. After about an hour of winding through the hills, her arms felt as though they were ready to fall off.

"How much further?" Erik wanted to know.

"Three or four more miles."

"When you're within a couple of miles, I'm going to jump out. I don't want you to stop, just slow to a crawl."

"That's about all we're doing now," she commented as the roadster groaned and strained up the hill. "Why in the world are you going to get out?"

"I don't plan on being a sitting duck. I'll get out and circle around and get the drop on old Hod just in case he pulls anything funny."

Tessa wasn't sure she agreed with this plan. "How will you know where to find me?"

"I just told you I was in the war, remember? Besides the smell of sour mash carries for over a mile."

But before he could carry out his plan, Tessa felt the car slipping off to the side as though it had a mind of its own. There was nothing she could do to stop it. She tried putting it in reverse to rock it out, but it was hopelessly mired.

"Don't rev it too much," Erik warned her. "We want you to go to Latham, not have him come out here with a welcoming committee."

"It's not much further." She reached over to get Pastor's rubber galoshes. "Maybe this slowdown will allow the agents to get here faster."

The back door opened. "I'll come through the woods, Tessa, and you'll not be out of my sight. Just remember that."

And he was gone.

Fighting down the acid taste of fear in her mouth, she pulled on the big galoshes and firmed the metal fasteners snug. Then she set out on foot. The snow was deeper here than out on the level. She'd nearly forgotten how lovely a walk through the hills could be. Looking out through the dense brush brought a rush of memories of her and Berg chasing and running wildly through the trees together. If anything happened to her, she and Berg would be together once again.

Her fingers and toes had lost their feeling when finally she topped a ridge and saw the dilapidated cabin tucked into a shallow valley below. A thin curl of white smoke rose up from the chimney. The gray-board shack beside the cabin housed the large moonshine still. And Erik was right—in the clear cold air, the unmistakable odor of sour mash was everywhere.

As she left the road and struck off across the clearing, Hod emerged shotgun in hand, from the front door of the cabin as though he'd been watching the road for her. He reached over and leaned the shotgun against the doorframe. Tessa had tried desperately to steel herself against this moment, but the very sight of him set her to trembling.

Erik's watching, she reminded herself. *Erik's right out there in those woods.* Stoically, she placed one foot in front of the other.

As she came closer, Hod pulled off his greasy hat and gave her a stained-tooth grin. His dark hair was askew as though it had never seen a comb. "Ralph was right on the money," he said, more to himself than to her. "He done told me if we put the feller in the clink, you'd come running to me just to get him sprung. He was right as rain." He chortled over his little victory. "Yessir. Right as rain."

When he took a few steps to meet her, Tessa noticed the limp. He reached down to rub the leg. "Yore ignorant boyfriend liked to broke my leg clean off me. Hurts like the dickens. Not a very nice feller what runs people right off the road."

Tessa stopped a few yards short of where he stood. She could go no further. Hadn't she done enough? Where were the agents? Her heart was thudding against her chest loud enough for the whole world to hear. She glanced at the cabin wondering if the man named Ralph was inside. Surely he wouldn't be dumb enough to be alone when she came. Did he suspect anything?

"Ain't you gonna come on over here and give yore husband a rightful hug? Doggone it, I most nearly forgot how purty you was. It about knocks me clean off my feet just to look at you." He spit a stream of tobacco juice, yellowing the white snow.

All right agents, her mind screamed. *Time to come out.*

Slowly he limped closer to her and she could smell the stench of his unwashed body. Shuddering she remembered the night in the rainstorm when he attacked her. Even the pouring rain couldn't dilute that horrific smell.

He reached out and pulled the muffler off her head. "Did you take out them braids just fer me?" He stroked her long curls with back of his hand. "I never did like them tight old braids. This is nice. Loose and all a-flowin' like this."

His hand slowly moved around her neck to pull her to him. She tightened. His face with the hooded eyes and tobacco-stained teeth was so close she could feel his breath. She did not move.

The sharp retort of a rifle ripped through the cold clear air. "Federal agents, Latham," came the shout from the woods. "Put your hands in the air."

Chapter 19

Hod's arm, strong as a tree trunk, spun her around and snugged her back against his chest. With lightning speed he yanked his hunting knife from its sheath on his belt and pointed it at her neck.

"You filthy feds want her alive? Then come out here in the clearing and throw down your guns."

Three men, dressed in tan hunting garb, came into the clearing. Tessa stared at them. If only they'd arrived a minute sooner. Surely there were more than three.

"Throw them guns down," Hod ordered again. "Then you high-tail it on outta here and leave me alone. I ain't done nothing wrong."

Tessa could hardly breathe with his giant arm across her chest. Her head was turned and out the corner of her eye, she caught a flash of movement. It was Erik scooting on his belly through the brush up toward the cabin. When he caught her eye, he motioned her to bite and then drop.

Hod hadn't seen him. His gaze was fixed on the agents as their rifles clattered into the snow.

Suddenly Erik sprang to his feet with a blood-curdling scream. At that moment, Tessa bit Hod's hand as hard as she could. As he recoiled from the pain, she dropped straight to the ground and rolled. Erik made an amazing football tackle sending Hod sprawling and the knife flying.

Hod writhed on the ground and groaned as he attempted to nurse his wounded hand and rub his game leg all at the same time. "My leg!" he wailed, "I think you done broke it."

"I can only hope so," Erik answered dryly.

Suddenly everyone was talking at once. One agent handcuffed Hod while the other two went to check out the still.

"There's enough evidence in here to put the guy away for a long time," one of them shouted out. "Who has the camera?"

Erik came to where Tessa was sitting in the snow and gave her a hand up. "Look there coming through the brush," he said with a grin. She whirled around to see Gaven racing toward her.

"Gaven!" she shouted. And with galoshes flopping she ran into his arms. She clung to him not daring to believe he was truly there with her.

Over and over he whispered her name into her hair as he held her tight. "I'm here, Tessa. It's all right. It's all over."

Slowly they walked arm-in-arm to where Erik was standing grinning at them. "Ah true love." He put his arm around Gaven's shoulders. "Say buddy, were you in time to see my great tackle?"

"Their truck bogged down just short of where you left my roadster," Gavin explained. "Then they ordered me stay back out of the way until it was safe. I didn't see much of anything."

"We'll tell you all about it later," Erik told him. Then to the agents he said, "I left one of Hod's partners out there in the woods tied up." He nodded in the direction of his little ambush.

"What pardner?" Hod said as he spat a stream of black tobacco juice. "Ain't no pardner of mine up here."

The agents looked at one another. "Say, where's Izzy?""He told us he was going to circle around. You don't suppose..." Looking at Erik, he said. "Was he a little guy?" He stuck out his hand to indicate the height.

Erik's fair complexion sported a blush as he nodded. "Short and strong as a bulldog."

"Oh my gosh!" said the agent. "Lead us to him."

Leaving one behind to guard Hod, they raced to keep up with Erik as he darted in and out through the trees. Tessa gasped as she saw the sight. There was poor Izzy, sitting on the ground tied to a tree, and gagged with a handkerchief. He was shivering horribly.

"We learned in the army to always carry rope," Erik said sheepishly as he untied the gag. "Sorry, pal. You sure do look like a fella from these hills. Great disguise."

Tessa too was amazed at how different Izzy appeared. She wasn't sure she would have recognized him herself. Dressed in a dark wig, weathered boots, and ratty-looking jacket and hat, he looked quite at home in the Oklahoma hills.

"I've been warned these disguises might cause me trouble one day," he said, rubbing his wrists as Erik untied him. "Now I think I have to agree." He looked up at Erik. "I thought *you* were one of Latham's men."

"Well, then," Erik said with a slow grin, "I'm glad I got the drop on you first. You might be good at disguises, but you don't know much about the woods. I heard you thrashing around about a mile off."

The good-natured Izzy only laughed. "You're probably right. But I had no time for a crash course on wilderness survival."

Although chilled to the bone, Izzy seemed none the worse for the attack from Erik who was almost a foot taller. As they tramped through the thick underbrush back to the cabin, they were all laughing at Erik's blunder. Everything suddenly seemed funny, gay, and happy. Tessa felt almost drunk with relief that it was all over.

The agents took photographs of the moonshine still, then proceeded to rip out the copper tubing and coils while a disgruntled Hod looked on. "That's enough for now," Izzy told them. "We'll send a crew out here in a couple of days to cart this off. Meanwhile let's get this John Barleycorn to the clink." He gave the handcuffed Hod Latham a shove in the direction of the road.

The vehicles were pushed out of their resting places in the snow-filled ditch. Hod was forced into the back of the old truck which had been driven up by the agents. One of the men crawled in behind him.

Gaven and Tessa shook hands with Izzy Eisenbaum. "Will we see you again before you leave Oklahoma?" Gaven asked him.

Izzy shook his head as he snugged his tattered overall jacket up around his neck. "Doesn't look like it. Soon as I take care of everything at the courthouse, I'll hop a train back east."

"Thanks for coming all this way," Tessa said.

"Don't mention it. I wouldn't have missed it. Nothing I like better than smashing a moonshine still. Besides, I wanted to tell my kids I've been to Will Rogers' country—way out west." He climbed into the truck cab. "Now I just want to get into my own warm overcoat." He waved as they drove off down the road.

Erik offered to drive the roadster back down out of the hills. Gaven gladly accepted, and Tessa snuggled up against him not wanting to ever let him go.

A joyous reunion was held at the Stedman home. The girls were jumping up and down and squealing. Pastor was slapping Gaven on the back, and Mama and Edith joined in the hugging. Edith insisted they stay the night and she would put supper on, but both couples were more than ready to head back home.

"We'll be back in a week for Thanksgiving," Gaven told them. "We'll have our celebration dinner then. All I want now is to get back to Tulsa, and back to my classroom."

As they left, Gaven couldn't stop thanking everyone for helping—for the visits, for the food. Thanking Erik for taking care of Tessa. Thanking Tessa for standing with him. Thanking her for putting herself in danger and on and on. Tessa had never seen him so animated, so alive.

As they drove back to Tulsa, following closely behind Erik and Clarette's Model T, he said, "Tomorrow after school, I'm going over to Elwood Street. If that upstairs apartment is still vacant, I'm putting down a deposit."

Chapter 20

"I know I shouldn't be bitter," Tessa said to Chloe, "but for Henry Patton to veto my application to the university..." She stopped and shook her head.

"You sure he done it?" Chloe wanted to know.

"Dr. Misek told us himself," Gaven said. "Henry Patton is one the biggest benefactors to the college."

They were sitting around Mama Sue's living room talking. The icy December chill was seeping in through the parts of the house, which hadn't been completely repaired. Sleet had been falling for the past few hours and now a major ice storm was underway.

Mama Sue was filling mugs with hot coffee. "So you just ask the professor flat out?"

Gaven nodded, holding out his mug for a re-fill. "After Thanksgiving, Tessa and I were talking, asking ourselves over and over why her application had been denied. It made no sense. Then I said, 'Why wonder? Let's just ask.'"

Preacher Sam shifted his position on the couch making the springs creak. "The professor wasn't afraid to tell the truth?"

"As a matter of fact," Gaven said, "Dr. Misek was very open with us."

"He asked me what I had done to offend the Mr. Patton so," Tessa said, trying not to grit her teeth as she said it. Ever since she'd learned the truth about his interference, she struggled with anger against the whole Patton family. They'd caused her nothing but grief. Now this.

"They's other colleges," Chloe offered.

"That's part of our plan," Gaven said. "I'll finish out this school year at Riverview, then we'll move to Stillwater. There'll be no Pattons there."

"I can get my degree at the state university with no interference," Tessa added, staring at Mama Sue's scrawny Christmas tree standing in the corner.

"Mmm," Mama Sue grunted her approval. "Right smart thinking. They need teachers there, too, Mr. Gaven. You get you a good job there."

Tessa jumped as sound of shouts and laughter from outside interrupted their conversation.

"Don't pay no mind," Chloe said. "Just them revelers. They think it's big fun to come speeding through here scaring the daylights out of folks."

"Surely they aren't destroying tents in this weather." Tessa couldn't imagine anything more cruel.

"No more of that foolishness, thanks be to God. Just hollering and carrying on like wild people." Mama Sue stood and headed toward the kitchen. "We gots a lemon cake out here. Any takers?"

"I'll help." Tessa followed her to the kitchen.

As Mama Sue cut the pale yellow cake, Tessa placed slices on the mismatched saucers.

"Mama Sue, remember when you and I talked about roots of bitterness and how they can grow?"

"Sure I remember. I told you how I plucks 'em out when they's little and easy to pluck."

"I think I've let a root grow pretty big."

"Now don't tell me. Just let me guess. Could it be someone with the last name what starts with a P?"

Tessa nodded. "And not just one—Trevalene and Sadella as well."

"Honey, don't do you no good to be hating them folk."

"I don't really *hate* them..." she started.

"Just give it a little time." Mama Sue shook the knife in midair. "If you let it keep on growing it'll soon be hate."

Tessa nodded. She knew that was right, but Henry and Trevalene had caused so much misery. "It's strange, Mama Sue, but it's easier to forgive Hod Latham." She held out another plate and Mama Sue placed a large slice on it. "After all, Hod is Hod. Never changed. But the Pattons are..."

"Devious?"

"That's the word. Their good side looks so good."

"Jesus done run up against that same problem with them Pharisees, honey. But he still forgive 'em." She waved the knife again. "And if Chloe done forgive them Pattons for killing her boy, you can do the same."

"I've been angry at them ever since..." She gave a little shrug. "I'm not really sure how long."

"If you don't forgive 'em, you is shackled to 'em. Did you know that?"

"I know. And I don't want that. What should I do?"

"Honey, the Lord can't do nothing till you're plum ready to give it all over to Him."

"The load is heavy, Mama Sue. I don't want to carry it any longer."

"Wanna pray now?" She lay down the crumb-caked knife.

Tessa nodded and held out her hands for Mama Sue to take. "Please."

———— ◉ ————

BY THE TIME TESSA AND Gaven were ready to leave, the sleet was pinging down and the ground was a glaze. He took her arm to steady her as they walked to the car, then gently helped her in.

"Be careful on your way," Chloe called out from the back door.

"We will," Gaven shouted back as he started the car. He guided the roadster carefully through the icy back streets of Greenwood. "Hey, this is like a skating rink," he joked. As he spoke, headlights appeared ahead of them, weaving crazily from one side to the other.

"Better get off to the side," Tessa said, "they're probably drunk."

About a block behind the first car, a second car followed. It too was weaving. Tessa wondered if they were purposely playing on the slick roads. "That's so dangerous," she muttered under her breath.

Gaven slowed and moved over to give the weaving car wide berth. Suddenly the car coming at them was spinning on the ice like a fancy-stepping skater. At the last moment the car reeled and skidded away from them to the opposite side of the road.

Tessa remembered screaming as she watched the car slam with a loud crash into a newly-set telephone pole. Now they could see clearly—it was Shelby's Silver Kissell.

Gaven shut off the motor and jumped out. "Stay here, Tessa. It looks bad."

"I can help." She slid over to get out behind him. Even though the road was rough and unpaved, it was still so slick she could barely stand.

Those in the car that had been following, had to have seen the wreck, but they weren't willing to stop and help. The car turned around and sped away, slipping from side to side on the icy road.

Tessa heard cries on the other side of the car. "You check on Shel," she said. "I'll see to the passenger."

In the darkness she could make out a girl in a tight-fitting shimmery dress, lying on the ice and crying in pain. Tessa pulled off her coat and spread it over the girl. "Lie still, Sadella. It's all right. We'll get help."

"Where's Shel? Where's my Shelby?"

Then Gaven was there. He pulled off his coat to put over Tessa's shoulders. "Stay with her and don't move her," he said. "There are no phones around here. I'm going for help."

Looking up at him, she asked, "How's Shel?"

Gaven shook his head. "Gone."

She gasped. "Are you sure?"

"The ambulance corps. Remember?"

She nodded. "Please be careful."

Gaven's roadster roared and was gone and she was alone with lifeless Shelby Harland in the car, and with Sadella's head cradled in her lap. Presently, Sadella's eyes fluttered open. "Shel? What did he say about my Shel?"

Rearing up and pushing out with all her strength, Sadella sent Tessa sprawling backward on the icy road causing a nasty bump on the back of her head. As she struggled to sit up, she saw Sadella crawling shakily to her feet and stumbling toward the wrecked Kissell. "Shel? Answer me, my darling. It's me Sadella. Shelby. *Shelby!*"

By the time Tessa could get herself to the car, Sadella was shaking the limp form of Shelby Harland, which was slumped over the steering wheel. Her pitiful screams split the cold night air.

Again, Tessa attempted to put her coat over Sadella's bare shoulders. "Sadella, come. Please sit down. You may be hurt."

But the girl was a wild woman. "You!" she shouted. "You're glad of this. Get *away* from me." Another forceful shove sent Tessa stumbling backward. Again, she hit the ground knocking the breath out of her.

"I can't live without my Shelby. I won't!" The words tumbled out in an incoherent babbling. "No, no, no. I can't, I can't." Tessa heard a crunching sound. The girl was wrestling a jagged piece of broken glass from out of the splintered windshield.

Tessa made a dive for the car but not before one of Sadella's wrists was gushing blood everywhere. "Stop!" Tessa screamed. "Help! Someone help us!"

Then the wild girl with glazed eyes turned on Tessa coming at her with the glass-spear weapon raised high. "You little witch," she cried. "Always in my way. Always interfering. I'll take you with me." Sadella lunged at her with the sharp glass cutting into Gaven's coat. As she did, Tessa put her head down and aimed for the girl's midsection upsetting her and knocking her to the ground. The moment she landed, Tessa was on top of her pulling the jagged glass from her grasp.

"Tessa! Is that you there, Tessa?" Willard was holding up a flickering lantern. Chloe was right behind him.

"Bring bandages quick. Sadella's cut her wrist."

Chloe ran to the nearest tent and came back with strips of cloth. Tessa kept the girl pinned down, not knowing what to expect next. Sadella was fighting for all she was worth with blood splattering everywhere.

"My goodness, girl," Chloe scolded, "What you do this for?"

Sadella struggled to pull her bleeding arm away. "Keep your hands off me, Chloe Franklin! I don't need your help."

"You done eat up with foolishness," Chloe said calmly. Then she firmly took the hand and skillfully wrapped the wrist while Willard pressed on the artery to slow the bleeding. As the bandage encased her wrist, growing crimson from the open wound, Sadella finally ceased her struggling and gave in to trembling and sobbing.

———◦———

TESSA HATED THE TASTE of coffee, but it was the only thing they had to offer in the hospital waiting room and she needed something hot. Even snuggled in Gaven's arms, she wondered if she would ever get warm. The leather-covered settee was none too comfortable. Her body ached from having been slammed around a few times on the frozen ground, and her bandaged hand throbbed. Sadella had been safely loaded into the ambulance before Tessa realized her hand was cut. Probably happened when she wrested the glass from out of Sadella's hand.

Tessa stared at the ragged rip in Gaven's overcoat and the bright blood stains, trying to comprehend all that had happened. Because of drunken foolishness, the only son of oil magnate, Elmore Harland, was dead. No war. No violence. Just plain old empty-headed foolishness. It made no sense.

Both Gaven and Tessa glanced up as a slump-shouldered Henry Patton came into the waiting area. His dull eyes scanned the room until he saw them sitting there. He'd obviously pulled on clothes in a hurry. No tie. No starched collar. No gold pocket watch. No spiffy matching vest. As Tessa watched him approach, she was surprised to realize she had no anger toward him at all. She felt only sorrow and compassion for the man.

"How's your daughter?" Gaven asked.

Henry dragged a chair closer to the settee and sat down. "They've given her something to help her sleep." He leaned forward with his hat dangling in his hands. "They say she'll be fine." He cleared his throat. "Physically anyway."

Tessa wasn't sure what to say. She felt Gaven tighten his arm about her shoulder.

"Trevalene's with her now. I..." Henry started, then faltered and started again. "I don't know if Sadella truly loved Shelby Harland, but I guess it's the closest she's ever come to loving anyone. Anger has boiled inside that girl nearly all her life. She's pretty broken up. It'll take time."

He blinked his eyes hard to squeeze back tears. Reaching in his pocket for a handkerchief, he realized there was none. Gaven offered his and Henry thanked him. "Elmore is devastated," he went on, seeming to want to talk about it. "Absolutely devastated. I guess neither he nor I have fared too well in the child-rearing department."

Tessa wanted to remind him that he had two younger children who were delightful and loving children, but she kept still, waiting.

Henry looked at Tessa through red-rimmed eyes. "I'm told you helped to save Sadella's life."

"Willard Franklin knew how to stop the bleeding," she offered. "Chloe wrapped her wrist."

"But you prevented her from..." He couldn't finish. "And she's nearly twice your size." Swallowing hard, he said, "I want to somehow thank you." With Gaven's handkerchief, he pressed at his eyes again, but the tears were coming faster than he could wipe them away.

"I think the city council is planning to incorporate your suggestion, Miss Jurgen. To have volunteers help process the building permits for Greenwood." His voice broke. He paused and swallowed hard. "I feel sure they can be processed more quickly." He scooted back the chair and slowly rose to leave.

"And one more thing. Your application to the university is being approved." He replaced his hat and touched the brim. "As it should have been in the first place." At the door he paused and turned. "Your scores were excellent."

Silence hung thick in the sterile waiting room. There was nothing more to say. The weary Henry Patton turned and walked away down the hall.

Tessa buried her face in Gaven's chest and let him hold her close.

"I knew it all along," he said in a whisper.

"Knew what? About Mr. Patton?"

"No. About you."

"What about me?"

"I told you the compassion inside you was bigger than the bitterness, and I was right."

"Only because I prayed, Gaven. Only because I prayed."

Chapter 21

"Hold still, child, or I ain't never gonna get this veil straight," Chloe said.

"*Ya*. Der twitching and der fidgeting help us none at all," Mama added.

"Whoever heard of having four mothers-of-the-bride?" Tessa said with an exasperated laugh. "This has to be the most crowded bridal dressing room in history."

Edith handed her the mammoth bouquet of red roses, with blooming lily-of-the-valley sprigs tucked in here and there. "One should be so blessed as you are."

"You would think she was complaining," Mina said. "Shall we all spank her?" Her remark brought even more laughter.

They'd been laughing and giggling most of the morning—a January morning, which dawned bright and clear. Even Clarette had joined in the gaiety and silliness.

"We could invite Mrs. MacIntyre in here, and then you'd have five mothers," Mina quipped.

"A fine gentleman, *Herr* MacIntyre is," Mama said, her Swedish taking over, "and kindly wife too. Growing family is truly a blessing."

Mama was right. The MacIntyre family was a delight and especially older brother Monty who took to teasing her immediately. And Gaven's mother had gently taken her aside last evening to apologize if she had sounded harsh over the telephone. Tessa felt sure the two of them would become fast friends.

Gazing at her reflection in the mirror, Tessa could hardly believe what she saw. Mama and Edith had worked miracles with the lace and satin. The elegant dress, arrayed in hundreds of tiny smooth seed pearls, was a perfect fit. The silkiness felt wonderful against her skin and made soft swishing noises with her every movement. She turned and gazed over her shoulder to view the long train as she gently fingered the pearls at her throat. Other than her ring, the pearls would be her only jewelry.

Suddenly the door opened and Vega stuck her head in. Her ruffled blue organdy dress was identical to Siegrid's. Both girls were wide-eyed with excitement. The visit to Tulsa alone would be adventure enough, but being in the wedding was almost too much. "The music's started," she said. "Please hurry."

"*Ya*, ve have ears and can hear," Mama told her. "You should be in line with Clarette and Siegrid." She waved her hand. "On with you now."

No sooner had she gone when a knock sounded at the door. It was Russ. "Hey, the ushers are ready to seat you fine ladies," he announced.

As the women left, Russ held out his arm for Tessa. She took it and together they walked down the church hallway to the foyer of the wood-paneled chapel. Soft winter sunshine streamed in from the tall stained-glass windows. Through the gauzy softness of her lacy veil she surveyed the small chapel filled with much of the population of Greenwood.

"At my wedding," she had told them, "no sitting at the back, or on one side. Sit wherever you please!"

Vega and Siegrid sprinkled rose petals down the aisle and took their places beside Clarette. At the altar, a beaming Pastor Stedman nervously smoothed his bushy mustache. Broad-shouldered Erik looked quite fetching in his new suit.

Then the organ music swelled, filling the room with warmth and golden joy. Black and white faces craned about to gaze at her, but only one set of eyes held hers.

Gaven, standing between Pastor and Erik, flashed her his wide warm smile, and his loving gaze carried her down the aisle toward him. Toward their new life together.

Norma Jean Lutz Bio

Norma Jean Lutz's writing career began professionally in the 1970s when she enrolled in a writing correspondence course. Since then, she has had over 250 short stories and articles published in both secular and Christian publications. The full-time writer is also the author of over 50 published books under her own name and many ghostwritten books. Her books have been favorably reviewed in *Affair de Coeur, Coffee Time Romance, Romance Reader at Heart, and The Romance Studio* magazines, and her short fiction has garnered a number of first prizes in local writing contests.

Norma Jean is the founder of the Professionalism In Writing School, which was held annually in Tulsa for fourteen years. This writers' conference, which closed its doors in 1996, gave many writers their start in the publishing world.

A gifted teacher, Norma Jean has taught a variety of writing courses at local colleges and community schools, and is a frequent speaker at writers' seminars around the country. For eight years, she taught on staff for the Institute of Children's Literature. She has served as artist-in-residence at elementary schools, and for two years taught a staff development workshop for language arts teachers in schools in Northeastern Oklahoma.

As a writer who loves writing for teens, and hanging out with teens, Norma Jean has launched the **Clean Teen Reads** website and blog. Lots of fun stuff for teens! Check it out here:

www.CleanTeenReads.net[1]

The Site for Teens Who Love Books and Stories

---

1. http://www.CleanTeenReads.net

Other Titles by Norma Jean Lutz

The Tulsa Series

#1 *Tulsa Tempest* (Christian historical romance)
#2 *Tulsa Turning* (Christian historical romance)
#3 *Tulsa Trespass* (Christian historical romance)
#4 *Return to Tulsa* (Christian historical romance)

The Norma Jean Lutz Classic Collection

1. *Flower in the Hills* (a sweet teen romance)
2. *Tiger Beetle at Kendallwood* (a sweet teen romance)
3. *Rockin' into Romance* (a sweet teen romance)
4. *Oklahoma Exile* (a sweet teen romance)
5. *Forever is Over* (a pre-teen novel about friendship)
6. *Lingering Dreams* (a sweet teen romance)

Teen Coming-of-Age Action Adventure Novels

Brought To You By The Color Drab
A Noble Cause: An Honorable Man Will Uphold a Noble Cause

Don't miss out!

Visit the website below and you can sign up to receive emails whenever Norma Jean Lutz publishes a new book. There's no charge and no obligation.

https://books2read.com/r/B-A-ZJGT-DEAYC

BOOKS 2 READ

Connecting independent readers to independent writers.